HOURS

11

HOURS

YAEL H. ZOUZOUT

authorHOUSE®

AuthorHouse™ LLC
1663 Liberty Drive
Bloomington, IN 47403
www.authorhouse.com
Phone: 1-800-839-8640

Published by AuthorHouse   06/05/2014

ISBN: 978-1-4969-1234-3 (sc)
ISBN: 978-1-4969-1235-0 (e)

Library of Congress Control Number: 2014908720

*Any people depicted in stock imagery provided by Thinkstock are
models, and such images are being used for illustrative purposes only.
Certain stock imagery © Thinkstock.*

This book is printed on acid-free paper.

Acknowledgements

I would like to express my gratitude to the many people who saw me throughout this book. To all those who provided support, talked things over, read, wrote, offered comments, allowed me to quote their remarks and assisted in the editing, proof reading and design.

My parents, my sister Hila and my brother David who encouraged me to indulge in my imagination. Above all, my mother who encouraged me and supported me, in spite of all the time it took me.

I would like to thank my grandmother and Aunt Lilas for not only motivating me with their curiosity, although also helping me get this book edited. My aunt Annatte for proof reading it with much care.

Thank you to the most incredible teacher Mrs. Benisti, for not only proof reading the book, although for also encouraging me throughout the years to allow me to attain my full potential. I hope I make you proud.

My high school friends, who enjoyed my electric ways and provided great suggestions.

A big thank you to my Yavne high school, for allowing me to become the person I am today.

Thank you to Author house, for publishing my book with great devotion.

Last but not least: I ask forgiveness of all those who have been with me over the course of the years and whose names I failed to mention.

For, Maman. Without your unconditional love, your unwavering guidance and support, all this could have never happened.

Chapter 1

At the edge of the ancient city sat a small house at the halfway point on Colle Street. Given its delightful beauty, this was a house that one would certainly not overlook. Not only was its appearance superior, but also the house had been constructed from notable material. An only child, Kate Tyler had the ideal luck of being born into a beautiful, wealthy family and to have extraordinary parents. As her circle of life completed its turn during her 11th year, Kate began planning a glamorous party. Purchasing amazing decorations, bright lights and beautiful invitation cards, she prepared for the event to take place on her birthday, the 29th of March. Kate was certain that this was going to be a celebration the likes of which no one had ever seen. All of the provisions were arranged. All she needed was for the guests to arrive.

It was now an hour before the party. Excitement flowing through her veins, Kate couldn't help but ask, "Are you sure people will come—" Before she was able to finish her sentence, the musical doorbell interrupted her. "It's probably Emily," she said as she ran to the door, trying her best not to trip over her extravagantly long party dress.

As she joyously welcomed Emily into her house, Kate felt as though her sister had arrived, as if Emily were part of her own family. The two girls had known each other for years now. Being in Emily's presence made Kate feel extremely comfortable.

The clock ticked. Half an hour passed. More people began to arrive. Each new guest boosted Kate's energy, especially when she noticed the fine packages they were carrying. This was a party that any kid would dream of having. The entire room was decorated in pretty, pink wallpaper covered with lilac fabric, which gave it a cozy look. The dining room table had been nicely set with a fuchsia tablecloth covered with small pink petals that made it look princess-like. Also on the table was a beautiful, three-layer cake covered with white and pink frosting. The most preeminent and breathtaking feature of all was the spa sitting in the corner of the house. Professionals, hired by Kate's parents for this occasion, asked each girl which treatment she wished to experience during the party. At seven o'clock, the sun began to set, leaving the girls anxious and not wanting to leave. After seeing their uneasy faces, Kate reassured them that next year she would host another extravagant party. Within the next 20 minutes, the girls left the house empty.

"Thank you so much, Mom, for the amazing party. I couldn't have wanted anything more," Kate addressed her mother while also yawning.

"My pleasure," said Isabella, kissing her daughter on the forehead. "Well, I better get to bed. I start school pretty early tomorrow." Once upstairs, Kate's thoughts were soon interrupted when the door opened a crack.

"*Daddy!*" Kate jumped on her father, gripping him in a massive hug. His response was simple: he handed her a beautiful jewelry box. Smiling very broadly, Kate uttered a quick thank-you as she slowly unbolted the box. Its soft case made her yearning to find out what was inside even stronger. Once she opened it, she saw a beautiful heart-shaped golden locket. The two diamonds inset into the pendant made Kate's heart skip a beat. She opened the locket to discover what was inside. To her surprise, she found a beautiful portrait of her family. Awfully thankful, Kate offered her assistance in cleaning up the mess, although, oddly, the downstairs was already clean. Echoing numerous thank-yous to her parents, Kate was shocked to discover that the gift giving was far from over. Gregorio and Isabella had hired a helicopter in which they would all take a ride, so as to fulfill Kate's dream. They took the enjoyable two-hour helicopter trip, pondering the entire lit up city as they viewed it from the air. Once their journey came to its conclusion, Kate was filled with satisfaction when she learned that horses awaited them on the ground. Her family would ride these horses home. Kate felt thankful, but— as thoughts began running through her mind on the way home—she also felt suspicious. Why would her parents have done so much for her? Not liking feeling disturbed, she rapidly pushed those thoughts aside and enjoyed 'her' day, ending it with a simple thank you, which was very significant coming from an 11-year-old.

Their ride home was unforgettable. For the next day, Kate had set her alarm for seven o'clock a.m. However, she had slept too late and had to drag herself out of bed. She got dressed and ran downstairs to find a huge breakfast laid out on the kitchen island. Isabella had personally prepared this meal for her daughter. The mere sight of the breakfast alerted and awakened

Kate. She was barely able to finish a quarter of her breakfast when she heard her driver honking outside, signaling that it was time for her to depart. The young girl gave her mom a quick kiss and made for the door after being sure to give her mother an extra hug.

The whole way to school, Kate's thoughts kept returning to why her parents were acting strange. Before she was able to seek the answer, she found herself standing in front of Filbert School.

Kate had valued this school ever since her first day of attendance. She was a wise student, frequently surrounded by blissful friends—especially today, the day after the notable party she had been fortunate enough to host. "Hey, Kate, what's doing?" Emily called out from behind her.

"I was just thinking of how amazing my party was," Kate said rapidly to excuse her unusual behavior.

"Yeah, I already told my mom all about it. She said that if I behave, I'll also have a party . . . with a spa," Emily said with a huge smile on her face. She lifted her head, envisioning how amazing it would be. Her best friend tried to look happy, although her thoughts had taken over her. As a close friend, Emily knew Kate like her pocket. "What's the matter? You don't seem too good. What happened?" Before Kate was able to respond, the bell rang. The girls each went to their classes. Kate heard Emily call out from behind her. "I'll catch you at lunch."

At lunchtime, Emily and a couple of friends had saved Kate a seat at their table. They all sat there with quizzical looks on their faces, finding Kate's attitude to be a strange one. After what they had witnessed last night, they could see no reason for Kate's anxiety. The girls cracked jokes and recounted humorous stories, which had a bit of a calming effect on Kate she then decided to enjoy the rest of the day. Emily couldn't help but wonder, *what had happened to my best friend?* After hesitating a moment, Kate told her that she felt weird and that something was wrong. "I had that when I turned 11, too. You feel weird since your body isn't used to being so big. That's what my mom told me," Emily said while intensively chewing a straw. After those words and a few more girls' opinions about her weird feelings, Kate completely forgot about the butterflies in her stomach. The rest of the day went by very smoothly. Kate had an

English test, which was tremendously easy, as Kate had always been a straight-A student. Tests weren't a problem for her; she nailed every single one.

The girls of Filbert School had one more recess before the school day was over. Filbert finished later in the day than all of the other schools in the city. Kate never liked that. Still, this was a private school with an outstanding reputation. The last recess of the day was always the most enjoyable. The students enjoyed playing numerous games on the large playground the school had generously provided. After competing in these games, they completely forgot that they were still in school until the bell reminded them. They each hurried off to class in high spirits. When the final bell rang, they left their classes, tired as usual. They all patiently waited for their drivers to arrive to take them home. As Kate stood at the entrance of the building, she waited for the white car to pull up in front of her, as usual. The second she stepped foot out of school, however, she was surprised to find that it wasn't going to happen like that today. Strangely, she was one of the last ones to arrive home. Once her driver, Zac, had finally appeared, he got out of the car, opened the door and apologized for the delay, saying that he had been with Kate's father. Once home, Kate found that she was starving and craving her mother's mouth-watering food. She enjoyed anything that was grilled, including hamburgers, chicken, vegetables and her favorite: steak. She hoped that her mother had made her steak. Calling out to her mother, Kate waited for a kind reply. All she heard in response was silence. She tried again. "Hi, Mom. I'm home."

Silence.

She wandered around the house, finding her father sitting at their sizable kitchen table. He was pale. Kate couldn't tell if this was because of sadness or fright. Her father was holding a large white envelope that seemed still to be sealed.

"Dad, why aren't you at work? You're never home this early. What's happening?" she asked, not sure that she wanted an answer.

While her father looked graceful sitting there at the table, he lifted his head and replied, "She's gone! . . . Mom's gone!"

Chapter 2

At that moment, Kate's skin matched her father's: pale. They were both terribly frightened. Kate, for one, felt like hiding. With an emotion unknown to her building up inside, she felt like running far away, where no one would find her. Her thoughts were suddenly interrupted by her father, who tried to soothe and promise her that he would do whatever was necessary to find Kate's beloved mother and his wife.

At this point, all kinds of questions to ask her father were forming in Kate's mind. Finally, she burst out in tears, murmuring, "Where has she gone? . . . Why??" Her father, unable to reply, joined her in crying until he finally straightened the envelope in his palm and began reading what was written on the back.

Dear Gregorio and Kate,

I'm sorry that I had to take your wife and mother so suddenly, but you cannot say that I didn't warn you. The envelope that is right now between your fingers is the key to what happened to your wife and mother. This envelope will not open unless you perform the three tasks I arranged for you. Each time you perform one of these tasks, the envelope will open a bit of its own accord.

Gregorio took a sip of water, wiped his tears, took a few long breaths and continued reading.

You might think that this will be easy, but if you fail to perform the three tasks in 11 hours (to begin at 12 noon on March 31, 2011, and to end at 11 p.m. the same day), your dear wife and mother will never be in your presence again.

Sincerely,

Uncle Ednesto

Before Kate was able to ask who Uncle Ednesto was and why he wanted her mother, Kate's father began answering her questions, as though he had read her mind.

"Many years ago, your grandfather Carlos, your mother's father, held tremendous power in his hands. Your mother's family, the Muratis, have held this burden for many generations. Before your grandfather passed away, he gave all his power to Mom, since he hadn't had a son. Now, Carlos had a brother," Gregorio paused for a few moments, exhaling loudly, "who is Uncle Ednesto."

When Kate heard that name the second time, shivers began crawling down her spine. She was aware that this was the devil holding her mother captive. Her father paused as well, not only to sip his cold glass of water, but also to swallow his pain. He let out a large sigh accompanied by a tear.

"Uncle Ednesto was always jealous of your grandfather, and now he is even more envious, knowing that the family power belongs to your mother. When you were born, Ednesto came to your first birthday party, claiming that if your mother didn't give him the power, he would murder the child. Your mother began crying and had begged him to take her instead. His response was, 'I'll be back in 10 years. And if you still refuse to give me your power, I'll take you and force you to give me your pride. And if you still refuse, the power will be destroyed. If I don't deserve to get it, then no one does.'"

Ernesto's voice rang in Gregorio's ears as if he had just heard it the day before. "Your mother and I hadn't believed him, although it would seem now that he has kept his word. I was at work when my office phone rang. I heard a loud scream and a kick, and then something shattered. I then felt someone on the other end of the phone (I guess it was Ednesto). He said in a deep, malicious voice, 'There's an explanation on the kitchen table.'" The envelope shook between Gregorio's fingers. "And when I got home, I found this."

Kate looked curious.

"What's in that envelope, in the first place, and what are the powers Mom has?" she asked, still with tears in her fearful eyes.

"According to my research, there are books stating that there is a certain breed of daunting magic called Abuha, which is a magic that charms envelopes, cards, letters and anything else made of paper. It then automatically gives the object the power to unlock doors to towers, buildings and the like," Mr. Tyler said, tucking the envelope into his pocket.

"You still didn't answer my question about what powers Mom has," Kate said anxiously, her beautiful, large eyes beginning to swell.

"Well . . . your mother has three powers: the power of speed, the power to change the weather and the power to manipulate fire—"

Kate interrupted. "That's why it's three tasks," she said, almost whispering, afraid to find out if this was true.

Nodding his head, Gregorio looked up and slowly uttered, "And, in case you were wondering, it's 11 hours for the 11 years of your life."

At this point, Kate just lowered her head. For the first time, she wished she was older.

Her father heaved a light suitcase onto the tabletop to remind her of what needed to be done next.

She ran upstairs and got what she needed: warm socks, a pair of boots, a hooded sweater, an extra pair of sweat pants, deodorant, a toothbrush, toothpaste and an extra T-shirt.

That will do, she said to herself. As her kind and loyal nanny entered the room, she saw Kate and instantly began to cry. Her eyes portrayed breathlessness. The nanny couldn't stop the wheezing sound from escaping through her teeth.

Catherine, employed by the family from the time Kate was born, was part of the family. Discovering that Isabella had vanished had an immense impact on her. "Thank you so much. It means a lot," Kate said in response to her nanny's empathy.

Catherine dropped what she had been holding and quickly rushed over to embrace Kate. After a long, emotional, dramatic scene, they both went downstairs to prepare the bag Kate had decided to take with her. While they were doing so, Kate apprehensively addressed her father. "Daddy, how will we know where to begin our first task, seeing as we weren't given any other information?"

Her father was busy with his thoughts and hadn't even heard his daughter's words. Kate repeated herself a few times until he finally responded. "At the top of the back of the letter, there is an address stating from where the letter had come. I'm assuming that that's where we start."

"Oh!" Kate said as she lowered her head. It was now 8 p.m., although it seemed much later to her.

The rest of the night was traumatic. As the minutes flew by, Kate studied her father as he packed a gold rhinoceros horn. He had discreetly set it aside, hoping that his daughter wouldn't discern its import. Kate thought that it would be better if she didn't press her father and instead allowed him to focus on more important matters: finding her absent mother.

*   *   *

All the way on the other side of the city, Ednesto sat in his overstuffed black leather armchair, enjoying a book about magic, when he heard a loud crying sound coming from the dungeons below. "Isabella," he whispered to himself in disgust. "Guards! Bring me my prisoner from the dungeons."

"Which one?" one of the guards asked, confused. The sorcerer held about 250 prisoners down there. Whoever didn't gratify him was detained as his captive.

Ednesto, a tall, black-haired man, got up and said, "You mean we have prisoners down there that are"—he paused—"still alive?" while laughing evilly. Then, Ednesto suddenly became solemn as he barked, "Isabella!" The guards rushed out. Before Ednesto had even had time to settle back into his chair and continue reading, the beautiful, blond-haired, blue-eyed woman was crying on the floor in front of him. "Very well, you may leave now," he said, satisfied, to the guards. Isabella struggled to get up, but the ropes tying her feet together prevented her. Before Ednesto said anything, he turned around, looked at her and laughed. He was finally about to get the family power in his hands.

"So, will the power be mine, after all?" he said while outstretching his arm.

"*Never!*" Isabella urgently replied to him, obviously in agony.

"Very well, then. Katy and Gregory will never be in your presence again," he declared while turning away.

"Yes," she said, still unable to stand. "Kate and Gregorio," she said, uttering their names correctly, "will be in my presence once again. You'll be surprised at what my family is able to do."

Ednesto walked around for a few minutes, as though unsure how to respond. Then, he lifted his index finger and placed it on his chin as he allowed a slight smile to slowly cross his face.

After a few minutes, the air separating Ednesto and Isabella became thick. When Ednesto finally sat, he said, annoyed, "Let's put it this way. I know that your family is very weak and will never be able to find you, but I still gave them a spark of hope. I gave them 11 hours to find you. If they don't find you in those 11 hours, not only will you not see your family ever again, but also you will never see daylight again," Ednesto said, laughing a most evil laugh. He was interrupted by his captive's soft sobbing. "What now?" he said, looking down at Isabella. "At least I gave your family a chance to—" Isabella was now struggling to get up.

When she finally did, she asked, "Are . . .
you . . . serious?" through gritted teeth. At this
point, she was very angry.

"Not only are you holding me captive
against my will, but you're not even giving my
family a chance to—"

"You don't understand, darling. I'm giving
them a chance, but if 11 hours is not enough,
that's not my problem," he rudely interrupted
her.

Isabella was now staring at him in
dismay. She did what any person in this situation
would do: she cried and cried for her family and
her safety.

"What will they have to do to get to me?"
she questioned, anxiously awaiting a response.

"Well, they've got three tasks to do, each
one aligned with your three powers. I will use
my sorcerer's skills to make the tasks appear.
The first one will be all the way in the north
of the city. They have to enter the tower and
make their way all the way up to the top of
it. Although, the obstacle which is waiting for
them, is one rare to compete with. This task will

align with your power of speed. An outstanding amount of animals will run at an uncontrollable speed around the tower on all the floors . . ." he paused. With a smirk, he said, "Wait. Why am I ruining it for you? You will watch it yourself. We have installed cameras in each of the three places where your family will be attempting the tasks. You will be able to watch the scenes for yourself."

Still staring at him, Isabella hesitantly asked, "What will be the second task?" She was trying to focus only on the future.

"You really think they'll survive the first assignment?" Ednesto said, aghast. Isabella had no time to respond, as Ednesto had commanded the guards to take her away. They dragged her, sweeping, on the marble floor of the large, enchanted house. Then they took her back to the dungeons' lowest floor, locking her in a room with only a bit of water for the next couple of hours.

*   *   *

"Time to go to bed. We've got a big day tomorrow," Gregorio said to his daughter while shutting off the light. Comprehending his message, she quickly ran upstairs. Ready to put on her pajamas, Kate became aware of a remarkable tune coming from her bedroom. The music was so beautifully composed, it seemed to drag her into the room. She hoped it would never stop. Following her eardrums, Kate came to an abrupt halt. In awe, she found herself staring at the most beautiful thing she had ever seen: a gold music box with blue designs on both of its sides and on the lid. Although the music box was open, all that was in sight was a beautiful violin, standing perfectly in the middle of some blue roses. Although Kate didn't know why, tears had begun to stream down her cheeks. She rushed to pick up the fragile box. Once the box was between her hands, a paper fluttered out of it. She read the following:

> Kate,
>
> When I was born, your grandfather Carlos (whom, I'm assuming, your father has already told you about) created this box for himself. This box is like a GPS, but a different type of GPS. This box cannot tell you where I am, although it can tell if I'm all right or, in other words, alive. My father always told me that this might come

in handy one day. I see now what he
meant. I want you to carry this box
with you wherever you go, wherever
my crazy uncle Ednesto will take
you. But remember, when the music
stops . . .

It seemed as if it has been hard for
Isabella to finish the letter to her daughter. She
signed off as any mother in this situation would
do, with this: "I love you, take care—and good
luck."

Kate felt scared and happy at the same
time, even though her mother was now standing
between life and death. She also knew that there
was beam of hope and looked forward to the big
challenge she would be facing tomorrow.

Kate was exhausted. She had just
managed to put her mother's music box in
her waterproof backpack (the music was still
playing, and Kate hoped it would play forever
and ever). Before long, the brown-haired,
brown-eyed girl was fast asleep in her queen-
size bed, oblivious to what awaited her in fifteen
hours.

Chapter 3

Snow filled the air; thick and fast, it rushed through the wide-awake city. It was now the end of March, when snow was uncommon. At the present moment, however, snow was here. A white blanket began covering the ground, the rooftops and the cars. Kate had always loved the snow. Because today would be a challenge, she awoke early instead of sleeping in, which she usually did on a snow day.

Kate arose to the sound of her father's footsteps creeping down the stairs. She tried to fall back asleep but just couldn't. She took a few moments to adjust herself to the rays of sunlight streaming in from the window across from her bed. Then she was wide awake. Kate slowly slipped out of bed and was heading to the bathroom at the far end of her room. Kate was a very lucky child. Her parents were both in business, which gave her the advantage of having a vast room that included a bay window, an expansive balcony, an immense walk-in closet and her own bathroom. She was a very lucky girl, indeed—that is, until yesterday.

She crept into her bathroom, not wanting her father to know that she was up. The night before, he had given her a speech about how important her rest was and about how the most important thing in the world for the Tyler family during the 11 hours awaiting them shortly was finding Kate's mother.

Before Kate brushed her teeth, she took a long look into the mirror, staring at her perfect cheekbones and her beautiful, painted-looking lips. She then gracefully caressed her striking, long brown hair. Her large brown eyes made Kate seem much older than she actually was. Analyzing herself, she tried to figure out what she had done wrong to deserve such a cruel punishment, although nothing appeared to give her an answer. When she finished brushing her teeth, she eagerly checked the time. It was already 10:30. She wondered when her father would come to wake her. She knew that her father had been right about needing her sleep. Fatigue began to dawn upon her, given that she hadn't gotten to sleep until midnight.

Well, it was too late now. All she could do at the moment was prepare for her only chance to find her mother. Her mom's life depended on the next 11 hours.

By the time the cook had finished preparing Kate's breakfast, Kate was ready and dressed to leave.

"So, are you ready to go, Dad? Come on!" Kate just wanted the 11 hours to pass already.

"It's only 11:15. Our three tasks begin at noon. Calm down; don't worry," Gregorio answered, trying to sound confident even though he didn't feel it.

Kate was about to answer when she let loose her tears, which streamed down her face. She was about to run upstairs when her father caught her arm.

"Eat. It will keep your mind off things. Please, for me."

Kate quickly gobbled down her breakfast. She felt so much stress that her palms were sweating. Also, she had little appetite.

At 11:30, Gregorio said that they should prepare to leave. As Kate arranged the suitcases in the car, she discovered a small white paper on the passenger's seat. She unfolded it. In bold handwriting, it read, "5958 Clusterstorm Avenue. Task one."

Kate rushed inside the house and threw the piece of paper at her father, eager to know where Clusterstorm Avenue was.

Before Mr. Tyler responded, he looked at the address for several minutes. He then examined the paper, turning it over a few times. He finally said, "This is where we have to go. It's way north of town. Just to get there takes half an hour."

Kate didn't let her father continue. She rushed to the door, saying, "Then, let's go! We haven't got a lot of time."

Her father quickly threw on his coat, put on his shoes and made for the door. When they were both in the car and ready to leave, Kate thought about the music box and quickly told her father that she had forgotten her backpack. It was in her room, she said, and was very important. She hurried to get it. Once she returned to the car, they were finally ready to go. Exactly at that second, their 11 hours had begun.

The drive all the way up north was hard and exhausting because, just a few hours prior, a huge snowstorm had flown across the city. Thankfully, the storm had ended, although it did leave quite a few piles behind. Their journey seemed that it would never end. Their dear cook, Annie, had supplied them with a basket full of a variety of delicious foods. Annie was a very talented chef who had worked all over the world and had been privileged to cook for the queen, the president and a few movie stars. Now, she was cooking for the Tyler family. After Kate had finished eating from the basket, her father pulled a watch from his pocket and handed it to her. He was wearing one just like it. "Here," he said, tossing it to her.

Kate took the navy-blue sports watch, studied it and learned that it didn't indicate the time.

"I programmed this timepiece. It will tell us exactly when the 11 hours are over," her dad said.

Kate looked at the object now strapped around her wrist. Time was going by fast. She had started giving up hope of finding her mother when her father disturbed her thoughts by

asking her to retrieve a CD from the suitcase—
one he had packed because music was one of
Kate's favorite things in the world. She had
loved music so much that her passion led her
to learn the most beautiful instrument in the
world: the violin. As Kate searched for the CD,
from the corner of her eye she caught sight of a
little object way at the bottom of the suitcase. It
was the golden horn. She wondered what kind
of power the horn held, although she couldn't
figure it out. She held it in her palm. It was much
heavier than she had expected. She was so
tempted to blow it and see what would happen,
but her father seemed anxious to listen to music,
so she gently put the horn back in the suitcase
and took out the CD, handing it to her father.
The rest of the drive up north was quiet and
peaceful. Gregorio and Kate were now listening
to their second CD when and they had to pull
over for gas.

*   *   *

"No, no, no. Over there, you . . . ugh!"
Ednesto yelled at his servants as they were
trying to arrange the task for the Tyler's. The
poor servants had been working since 3:00 in
the morning. Ednesto performed magic again

and again to make sure that the place assigned as the Tyler's' beginning point was perfectly charmed.

Isabella sat in a small armchair in front of a large wooden desk. Ednesto stood in front of her, taping a small bottle onto her wrist: an hourglass.

"I have charmed this bottle, just as I have charmed many other things," the evil man said, laughing. "And, like I mentioned yesterday, as well as 10 years ago, if you don't immediately allow me to inherit your powers, then you will never again witness a sunrise. You still have 10 and a half hours to think about it."

"I know that no matter what happens, my father would never consent to your holding the family burden," Isabella quickly responded to her cruel uncle.

"Well, then. I see we're done here. There's nothing more I can do. And remember, the sand is making its way through the glass. The spell I cast that will bring about your death will automatically be activated," he said, turning his back and walking away.

Very soon, Ednesto was stopped by Isabella's small voice as it followed his footsteps. "Please, Father, help my family complete the three tasks safely . . . please." She then quietly sobbed to herself.

Ednesto smiled. Before he left the room, he turned around, a mocking expression on his face, and said, "Oh, I almost forgot the camera!" He then opened the curtain. There before Isabella's eyes, was a large screen, which had replaced the somewhat beautiful window she had imagined. Without saying a word, Ednesto took a remote control from his cape pocket and turned on the television. Isabella could barely keep her eyes open. She was too shaken by thoughts of the upcoming task her family would have to perform. Isabella quickly turned away from the screen, not wanting to think of watching her family suffer before her eyes. As she desperately tried to look away, Ednesto sighed in annoyance and lifted his finger. At that moment, the brightest light Isabella had ever seen rushed from Ednesto's fingertip as he moved her head towards the direction he wished it to be: facing the screen. She tried to resist, but Ednesto had enchanted her to do as he commanded.

Ednesto was about to leave the room when Isabella yelled from behind him, her head still. "You can't do this! You cannot just enchant things for your own benefit!"

Her uncle laughed. "I already did." Isabella couldn't understand why he wished to possess the power. Magic was supposed to bring joy and add life. It was certainly not intended to be used for one's own benefit. Thoughts fled through Isabella's mind as she tried to imagine what would become of the world if her uncle got what he desired. She had to ensure that he didn't.

Isabella then heard a door slam and managed to listen to Ednesto's quick footsteps down the long staircase. She pulled a picture from her pocket, her head, against her will, still fixated in the direction of the screen. She quickly replaced the awful view by holding up the most beautiful thing in the world to her: a photo. She stared into the brown eyes staring back at her. She saw a beautiful child smiling at her while a king of a man embraced the girl. Those people were her family, the people she loved. Soon, those same people would have to pass the gate and walk through the horrors of task number one.

Chapter 4

The tower on Clusterstorm Avenue was
something impossible to describe. The closer
Gregorio and Kate got to it, the tighter the knots
in their stomachs became. From the moment
they set foot on the grounds, Kate exhaled a
sigh filled with terror and despair. The 11 hour
countdown had already begun, and yet Kate's
emotions did not cease to build inside of her,
seriously frightening her. A dark-complexioned,
muscle-bound figure, 6 feet 4 inches in height,
begged for attention. Kate didn't have to look
twice to know that the man standing before
her was, indeed, Ednesto. His large, dark brown
eyes mirrored his dirty soul. They were truly
the windows to his soul, ones easily able to
send shivers down the young girl's spine. Solid
yet fragile, Kate had no choice but to drop her
gaze. The force was too strong for her; she
needed a way out. As thoughts began rushing
through her mind, culminating in emotions
she had never before experienced, the bold
man standing before her interrupted the stiff
silence. She shuddered. Soon, her lips began to
shiver and her arms began to sweat. "Pleased to
meet you. I am Ednesto," he said. With rage in
her eyes, Kate gazed sharply at her great-uncle.

Noticing her audacious behavior towards him, he smirked and gently but menacingly pinched her left cheek. She almost felt herself collapse at his touch. Gregorio and Ednesto exchanged a few brief words while Kate stared in complete disgust, afraid. Ednesto began by introducing what the two would experience over the dramatic course of the next 11 hours. His descriptions were harsh yet straightforward. The more he spoke, the more instructions he issued, and the more Kate felt the encumbrance on her back become heftier and denser. Shortly (although to Kate, it seemed like forever), the dark-skinned man ended his speech graciously and malevolently. Kate shivered as Ednesto walked away.

"Let's begin, Dad. We can do this!" The tower lay still before their eyes, although the more they gazed at it, the more they felt vertiginous. Animals were roaring, racing and flying by at an almost impossible rate of speed. "Let's do this!" Kate repeated, this time feeling more willpower.

It looked as though Ednesto had gathered together all of the animals in the universe, emptying out all the forests. This turned out to be a correct assessment; Ednesto had emptied out all the forests and zoos in town. But he hadn't just gathered all the animals; he had also manipulated them with magic, charming them to follow his commands. He told the Tyler family that their three tasks were based on the powers of the Muratis. Gregorio and Kate could see that Ednesto had kept his promise, the task clearly seemed undoable. Their first task corresponded with one of Kate's mother's powers: speed.

The animals, moving at reckless speeds, ran around the tower and on every floor. Kate and Gregorio couldn't stand still. Kate was brave and decided to advance a few steps closer to the tower. With fortitude, she accelerated her speed. When she could clearly see the tower door, Gregorio had no choice but to follow his courageous daughter. The closer they came to the entrance of the tower, the more their eardrums seemed to be bursting. The reverberation was so loud that Kate had to cover her ears. Then, Gregorio observed her slowly take her hands from her ears, as though trying to concentrate on another sound. Her head began moving from place to place, trying to locate the source. She opened her purse, seemingly searching for an object. When she finally felt what she had been hoping to find, a gleam appeared in her face. She quickly dug into her purse. Once she held the music box between her fingers, she gently lifted its lid. At that moment, a warm tear slid down Kate's cheek as she observed the beautiful violin surrounded by blue rose petals. The music was so beautiful, so striking, that it completely drew her in. She was about to close the lid, aware that she only had 9 hours and 45 minutes left to find her mom. Before she managed to close the box, however, she heard a voice come from the beautiful little object. "Don't be afraid. I'll protect you. Go!" She recognized that voice. It was her mother's! Kate was about to answer, but before she was able, she felt a cold hand on her left shoulder. At first afraid to lift her head to find out who it was, she did so slowly, only to discover that she was facing her great-uncle Ednesto. He looked at her with piercing black eyes, as though wishing to hypnotize her. If that was his intent, he hadn't succeeded.

After a long moment of confused silence, Ednesto said, almost in a whisper, "Will you be entering the tower, or did you drop out already?" He didn't have to wait long to receive a response. He was taken aback by Kate's rude manner of departing. Heading towards the animals, she was stopped by Ednesto's voice. "I'll be up in my tower watching your every move," he said, nearly disappearing. Then, he turned abruptly, as though he had forgotten to mention something important. He was now staring at Gregorio, whose eyes were on the speeding animals. "Don't think I'll be lonely up there. I have your wife as company," Ednesto said. Kate followed Ednesto's glance, which had fallen on the big watch hanging on a pole at the back of the tower. Kate had barely noticed it before. Her thoughts were interrupted by Ednesto's cold voice saying, "The clock is ticking. Remember, you've got only 9 hours and 41 minutes left." He then marched off, an evil laugh grumbling at the back of his throat. He cut a disturbing image. Still, nothing discouraged Kate, as the thought of her mother was with her.

Kate was half a foot away from the animals when she felt her father's hand on her elbow. "We can't just enter like that; we need first to create a mental act so that we don't get stepped on. While your head was doing whatever it was doing in that bag," he said, pointing to Kate's designer purse, which she was clutching tightly, "I was determining the method by which we will get in there." He took a crumpled piece of paper from his pocket. It showed a grid and outlined every moment of their journey up north to complete their task.

It also specified how they would receive the next clue, or whatever it was, to get closer to Kate's mom. "As you see, darling, the first floor contains every type of monkey in the world. We can manipulate them by doing ourselves what we want them to do. It is scientifically proven that monkeys have the ability to mimic humans. Eventually, we will make it through this chaos," Gregorio said. Kate just nodded, agreeing to her father's idea. With no time to waste, they moved closer to the monkeys until they were practically able to touch them. Father and daughter pair quickly began jumping around as a test, to see whether or not it was true that monkeys mimicked people. Sure enough, after a little while, Kate and Gregorio noticed a small monkey mirroring their every move. He was full of enthusiasm and jolliness. A few moments later, another monkey, standing beside the first, picked up on what the first monkey was doing and rapidly joined in as though a game had begun. Seeing this, Kate was immediately excited. Her father was nervous. Quickly, with great motivation and enthusiasm, the two put forth all the effort they could muster. They invented new, jolting movements to get the monkeys to separate, which would create a slightest opening and allow Gregorio and his daughter to enter the tower. After much concentration and calculation, they finally persuaded the monkeys to part, at which point Kate and her dad entered the tower. Almost instantly, they found themselves in a lift. It was small. Kate wasn't able to breathe.

*   *   *

In luxury, Ednesto sat in the opposite tower, watching his victims suffer. As he let out a slight chuckle, he was amazed by their apparent dread, agony and fear. In reality, this was only the beginning. This was just a taste, a preparation for task number two and three.

*   *   *

Intensely gasping for breath, Kate wouldn't allow this to be the end. She and her father were barely in the first hours and on the first task. A feeling of faintness overcame Kate. Her father tried to fan her with a receipt he had found in his pocket. By the time she recuperated and began breathing normally, the thick, crystal-clear glass opened. Kate fainted. This time, they didn't see cute monkeys jumping around. What they beheld now was the Madagascar crew. With hundreds of lions, zebras, hippos and giraffes speeding around them, Gregorio and Kate's fear spiked to a whole new level. After a few attempts to sparkling water on her face for her to awaken, she finally did. As she began gazing in awe, she noticed a shadow fly by. With the fear that there was no possibility of getting these creatures to mimic their actions. They needed to come up with a different plan. They needed some sort of tool. They needed magic. Many moments of silence passed before Gregorio gracefully took out a small silver wand from his satchel.

Chapter 5

"Smart family you got there. They might have been able to impress me by performing this first task—and maybe the next ones, too. Although the amount of time remaining is insufficient for them to complete all three." Ednesto paused for a moment, as though awaiting a response. He asked, "Don't you concur?" Ednesto hadn't even noticed that Isabella was affectionately staring at her family. He continued with his nastiness. Showing absolutely no concern for his niece's feelings, he pulled his watch from his robe and placed it before Isabella's wet eyes. At this point, nothing else could bother her. Seeing her family's enthusiasm to save her was touching—heartbreaking, even. Then, something she hadn't expected to see caught her eye . . .

* * *

Kate and Gregorio leisurely walked through a sea of elephants. The animals were dashing by so quickly that they barely noticed Kate and her father creeping against the walls of the tower to get to the other side of the stairs. Waiting on the other side of the second floor was a box that had been displayed to them for the past 45 minutes, since the time they had first arrived at this overwhelming skyscraper. It was small yet big enough to be noticed from the bottom of the tower. This box contained their "hint" to the next task, It had a long and daunting ordeal to bypass the animals. Although Kate was evidently protected by her mother, it did not diminish her determination. The fascinating music continued to warm her heart.

Kate was now almost at the steps reaching to the third floor. She walked slowly, feeling that someone just might slink up behind her. She was in front of her father when she caught a glimpse of a shadow. It took her some time to make out its shape, as the shadow kept moving. Every step it took triggered Kate's heart to skip a beat. The heavy atmosphere inside the tower was unpleasant and left her feeling frightened. Within minutes, Kate discerned that the shadow was in the shape of a man's body. Kate peered closer. She was wrong; it was a young man's silhouette. It seemed as though he was wearing a cape. She now moved faster, her curiosity pushing her to find out who he was and what he was doing in this tower at a dangerous time like this.

When Kate reached the steps, she jogged up them. Her father, not understanding why she was acting this way, for he had not seen the silhouette yet he followed her nonetheless. Once Kate reached the top of the staircase, she was blinded by an overly bright light that approached them from its source in the center of the room. It was beaming out of the box, the one she had seen upon first arriving. The thought most prevalent in her mind was learning more about the person who cast the mysterious shadow. She looked around herself some more, but the wraith was nowhere to be found. Kate's curiosity led her to move towards the box. Gregorio moved closer, too, showing Kate that he was now taking charge. He gradually struggled to approach, but the light was too strong for him. It was a thick cement wall separating him and his daughter from their next task. It seemed to Gregorio that he needed a secret code in order to get information about their next step. Kate noticed that the entire purpose of this evil scheme was to squander her and her father's time, perturbing them in their efforts to save Isabella. As if on autopilot, Kate's mouth began spilling words, which she hoped would dim the light and permit her and her father to access the box standing but meters away from them.

"I am the almighty Ednesto! Ednesto's the greatest. I've got the power." Before she was able to utter another one of her strange predictions about what the code or spell might be, her father gave her with one of those looks indicating that her guesses were getting them nowhere. Kate—a person who expects a lot from herself and believes that she is able to make anything happen if she wants to—was displeased that she couldn't get it right.

Gregorio was impatient with Kate's continuing efforts. He was certain that just standing there would impede their progress. "Katy, sweetie, pay better attention, will you?"

It had just occurred to Kate that her father had been talking for the past five minutes, but she hadn't been paying attention to him. Reflexively, Kate replied to her father, "Umm . . . sorry. I tried, I was listening." Her father just nodded. For a few long moments, Gregorio seemed to gaze into another world through squinting eyes, as though he were fighting the light pouring through. After several minutes, he spoke to his wide-eyed, worried daughter. "I have at last come to a conclusion. I can identify exactly what Ednesto's secret password is!" Kate jumped, amazed that her father had solved the problem. He seemed to be mechanically walking towards his answer. Behind the light was a small opening leading to the other side of the cement wall. "Can people in this world be any more cruel?" Kate asked. Since the time Kate had met Ednesto, she acknowledged that even the most evil minds can be wise. Kate was about to share her thoughts with her father when she noticed that he had already found his way through to the other side of the wall. Kate struggled through the blinding passage to reach her father. Once she got to the other side, she saw her father holding a small, elegant beige piece of paper. He was positioned next to the box which had, when they had first arrived to Clusterstorm, caught their eye. Now, Kate's desire to find out what was beneath the mysterious, carved wood was intense. The box was finally opened. She was content, acknowledging that she and her father would soon be approaching task number two.

"Is that our next clue?" Kate couldn't help but ask.

"Well, it's actually a riddle, which I'm assuming will lead us to our next clue to get close to Mommy."

Kate shivered the moment her father uttered that name. The last time Kate had said the word *Mommy* was two days ago, and she already missed it. "Well, then, let me see it." Kate was determined to find the answer to the riddle.

"It's pretty hard. I mean, I'm still trying to figure it out, so don't be hard on yourself," Gregorio said while hesitantly handing over the riddle to his daughter.

Kate read, "*I'm the part of the bird that's not in the sky. I can swim in the ocean and yet remain dry. I will lead you to your next destination. What am I?*" Kate lowered the paper then rushed to the window across the room. She quickly opened it and stuck her head out.

"Sweetie, this is no time to get some air. I told you it was hard, but we shouldn't give up already," Gregorio said encouragingly.

"Daddy, you know I'm not a quitter. I'm just trying to see what the riddle is. I'm looking for a bird so that I can determine what part of it does not fly." Gregorio was so proud of his daughter's bright idea that he rushed to the window to wait for a bird to cross over their heads. In no time, a bird did fly overhead. At first, they weren't able to perceive anything to help them solve the riddle. Once they peered closer, however, they realized what the answer was: the bird's shadow. *Of course! The shadow is the only thing that could remain dry,* Kate thought to herself as she looked closer at the bird's shadow, which seemed to be motioning towards something: a car across from the tower. Before the young girl broke her head trying to figure out how that car could possibly help her and her father and provide them with a hint about their next destination, she felt her father drag her down the steps. The tower had somehow become marvelous—glorious, even—without the daunting presence of the animals, who seemed eager to destroy it. Once Kate and her father had made it all the way down stairs, they were greeted by Ednesto's fake smile.

"I see you managed to get through the first task," he said, his smile fading. He quickly put on his 'serious' expression. "But don't be so sure that you'll succeed the second time." Kate who very angry, was tempted to answer with a rude comment. Just when she opened her mouth to spill the harsh words buried in her heart, Ednesto motioned her and her father to the car. They saw that it was a limo.

In less than 30 seconds, Ednesto disappeared from their sight. Gregorio rushed to open the door for his daughter so they could get going. Once in the limousine, Kate tried to see who the driver was, but the dark glass partition separating the front from the back prevented her. When the vehicle reached a corner, the driver turned his head. A beam of light shone from the window. Now, Kate could almost make out the figure. Once the beam positioned itself on the driver's eyes, Kate couldn't believe what she saw. It was the young man she had seen in the tower. He looked familiar, but she didn't know why.

Top of Form

Chapter 6

The limo came to a stop in front of an airport. Neither father nor daughter knew whether or not they should exit until the door opened. Kate assumed that the young man had opened the door, although she could not see his face clearly. He seemed to be wearing a hooded jacket twice his size, as if to keep his identity hidden.

When Kate and Gregorio finally stepped out of the vehicle, they noticed the young boy humbly holding out two plane tickets. Kate grabbed them quickly, curious to see what the next destination was. When she was able to make out the words printed on the tickets, her eyes widened. Her lifelong dream was to somehow end up in England—and these tickets were for a flight to the UK. "Maybe this isn't so bad," Kate said as she let her mind drift to other thoughts.

"Kate, how can you say that?! This trip is not a world tour; it's a journey to rescue your mother!" Gregorio said while shaking his head from side to side.

"You're right, you're right. I'm just trying to look at the positive, you know," Kate said, trying to hide her excitement. Fifteen minutes later, they were boarded onto a plane which allowed them to arrive to their destination in 40 minutes, soon enough they were off to their next task. Once the plane was in the air, Kate's boredom led her to explore her purse. She found a tube of lip gloss, a mirror, her iPod, sunglasses, her wallet and her camera—and then she dug deep in the corners of her purse. Besides the music box, which was playing its beautiful tune, she found the envelope, the one she and her father had received several hours ago. She examined the envelope, peering closer, and soon found that the right side of the envelope had opened. She quickly showed her father what she had just discovered. He was overwhelmed, seeing that they had finally accomplished something in this extremely difficult mission. It gave him a certain satisfaction, which brought out a smile on his dim face. The flight no longer felt that long, now that they had discovered that their hard work had paid off. As a reward, the envelope had opened some. Presently, all he yearned for was to fully complete the mission and rescue his captive wife.

Once the plane landed and Kate and Gregorio had disembarked, the young man reappeared to give them the next address. Kate was about to ask him who, exactly, he was, but he had quickly disappeared into the crowd, blending in with the tourists. She and her father were now in Teesside Airport just outside of Middleton, St. George. Kate got a glimpse of the directions her father was studying and saw that their next mission had something to do with a lake. She knew all the lakes in England. Now, she just wondered which one they were going to visit. She looked at her watch. They now had seven hours left.

"Let's go. We haven't got much time," Gregorio said to his daughter, dragging her by the hand. Once outside of the airport, Kate just stood there, mesmerized by the beauty of England. Kate had loved the country ever since she could remember. Its elegance had always attracted the beautiful 11-year-old. She knew everything there was to know about England: numerous historical monuments, national events and, most important, the royal family. Anything involving the queen and the graceful princesses and dukes aroused her excitement, although the source of her ultimate fascination was the British accent. She could listen to someone speak with that accent all day long.

"Kate? Kate? Kate? Kate?" Gregorio tried to bring his daughter back from her musings.

"Uh, yeah, sorry. Daydreaming. So, what now?" she quickly answered so he wouldn't pry into her private thoughts.

"Our cab's here. Let's go." Once they got into the car, Kate's father gave the driver the address. Soon enough, they were on the road. "So, Dad, where are we going? I saw that we're going to a lake. Which one?" Kate asked, looking out the window and admiring the historic monuments.

"Well, you saw right. We are actually now heading to Cumbria, where Windermere Lake is situated. According to my research, if we hit no traffic, we'll be there in exactly one hour and fifty-five minutes and—" Gregorio said, trying to sound interesting, before Kate abruptly cut him off. "Wait, did you say Windermere Lake?" Kate asked, turning away from the window to stare at her father. Her eyes lit up.

"Um, yeah . . . have you heard about it?" Gregorio asked as if talking about an object.

"Heard about it?! Dad, Windermere is the biggest lake in England. Oh my gosh, I can't wait. And, by the way, since when do you do research?" Kate said in a humorous tone while returning her gaze to the window so that she could enjoy the view she'd always dreamt of seeing. Kate let her father talk while she enjoyed breathing the beautiful England air.

*   *   *

"May all the passengers please board the plane. We will be leaving in five minutes. Thank you."

"Argh, it's already been twenty minutes since they said we'd board in five minutes. We have to get to Windermere before they do. If not, they won't take me seriously, and . . . and . . ."

"And, it's not we; it's you. I am refusing to enter this plane!" Isabella thought it was necessary to answer the evil man who was torturing her family. Even though she knew that Ednesto would get *his* way, Isabella wasn't stymied in defending the very little honor she had left.

"Ha-ha, you think you can make decisions! You are far from able, so get realistic." Ednesto's evil laugh made Isabella want to cry. But this time, instead of weeping, she lifted her head as though she hadn't heard him.

"You know, I've got more power. I can always make your head stiff again. I can do anything I want with you."

Isabella now felt strong enough to answer back. The flight attendant called out that it was time to enter the plane. "I guess you will be joining me, then," Ednesto said.

"Do I have a choice?" Isabella answered, annoyed.

"Not quite. Let's go," he said in a mean yet calm tone.

Ten minutes later, the plane took off. Because they were seated in first class, they were well served. During the plane ride, Isabella was only able to think the horrible situation currently confronting her family. She asked Ednesto, "So, what will this task require? Building buildings? Cleaning the lake? Or, perhaps, swimming across it?" She paused here, expecting her uncle to yell at her. She wasn't sure if he had heard her, so she repeated herself a little louder. Again, no effect, no response, nothing but silence. She touched her heart to make sure she was still alive. *You never know with Ednesto,* she thought to herself. *Well, then, I better benefit from this little bit of freedom,* Isabella concluded. She decided that if she couldn't see her family, she would contact them. "Perfect," she said under her breath. Then she pressed the button on her left armrest, the one marked with an icon of a woman. Not two minutes later, a flight attendant appeared with a menu, which she placed in Isabella's left hand. Then she handed Isabella a strawberry kiwi Snapple. "How can I help you, Madame?" the flight attendant asked. Isabella got up from her seat before answering the short, red-haired woman. She was careful not to wake Ednesto, who was napping. She was certain that with these free few moments, she would be able to try to get her family out of this mess.

I'm the one who got them into this disaster, and I'm the one who will get them out of it, she thought.

"Pardon me, what was it you wanted?" the little redheaded attendant uttered in a sweet voice, looking confused.

"Oh, nothing. It's just . . . well, do you, by any chance, have a phone I can use?"

Isabella saw that the woman was hesitant, so she flashed one of her irresistible smiles. Isabella was known for her ability to tempt people and lower their resistance with her smile. Just before Isabella was about to plead, she found herself being led to a door at the rear of the plane. "Make it quick. I'm not supposed to let anyone in here," the flight attendant said to her. Isabella was about to thank her when she disappeared behind the swinging door. Without wasting more time, she quickly dialed her husband's cell phone number. She waited through the first ring and then the second. Gregorio picked up on the third ring.

"Hello?" he said. Isabella was so excited that it took her a few moments to put herself back together. When she was able to catch her breath, she excitedly answered her husband.

"Hello!" She heard no answer. The line was completely quiet. "Greg, are you there?" Nothing changed this time. Silence was the reply once again. She was about to speak a third time when she noticed a dark, evil shadow behind her.

It was Ednesto. He was holding a pair of scissors in his right hand.

"Humph, did you really think you could outsmart me, young lady?" Even though the question seemed to be a rhetorical one, Ednesto demanded an answer.

"I'd really rather not answer that question," Isabella said.

Ednesto acted like he hadn't even heard her reply." I can't believe you" Isabella didn't even bother to look at or even answer him. She just left him standing there near the phone, swinging the door hard enough so that it would hopefully swing back and make him fall. After quickly doing so, Isabella got out of the way so that it wouldn't hit her.

All she heard at that moment was, "How dare you?" followed by a thumping noise. Isabella felt good that she was at least capable of showing her uncle what she was able to do.

*   *   *

Kate and Gregorio's long cab ride was finally coming to an end. Kate recognized their final destination when the driver turned onto the A592 Promenade. Kate was dazzled by the beauty of the city. The cab's GPS indicated that they had arrived at their destination. She and her father were finally standing before Windermere Lake on Glebe Road.

"Ah! I cannot believe we are finally here. It's so beautiful—and so much nicer in person . . . and . . ." Kate's voice dropped, and then she continued. "And look who's here on time." Ednesto quickly flashed a shiny smile, trying to hide that he was sweating and out of breath. Once he realized that he had no way to catch up with the Tyler's, he had chartered a small craft to take him to his final destination: Windermere Lake.

"We want to begin—or, should I say, end—this. Hand over our next clue!" Kate said to Ednesto.

"Pff, there's nothing to hand over. It's as clear as black on white. It's easy. All you have to do is cross the lake's islands and find the questions that will, once answered, reveal clues. The questions will be underneath rocks placed beneath trees. Each correct answer will lead you to the next island in the lake. I figure that you won't get lost with the help of the clues. Once you reach the final island, you will find a box that will only open once you speak your final answer to it. Now, I'm sure that you realized that each task corresponds to one of Isabella's three powers. This one has to do with the power to change the weather. So, be prepared. You never know what I'll shower you with. Get it? Got it? Good," Ednesto replied.

Kate felt dizzy. She didn't know how a human being was able to talk that fast.

"Hey, Katy, did you understand your great-uncle? I was lost after he said, 'It's easy.'"

"I'm with you, Dad. I got lost after he said, 'It's as clear as black on white.'" Gregorio now looked discouraged. Even when looking at his daughter's face, which was full of faith, he wasn't so sure of himself anymore.

Just then, the young mystery man walked up to them. This time, before Kate had the chance to ask him who he was, he introduced himself.

"Hello. My name is Ben Dingo."

Chapter 7

He was a tall handsome boy with messy dirty blond hair. His piercing ocean blue eyes were noticeable from afar, yet his smile gave him a very childish look. He seemed very excited to meet the Tyler family.

"Hello, I am Gregorio, and this is my daughter, Kate," Gregorio said while shaking the young man's hand. Still not sure of who he was, Gregorio, deep down, had a warm feeling about him.

"Oh, I'm sorry, let me introduce myself. I am Ednesto's trusted advisor. He comes to me whenever he needs something planned. I'm the one who planned out your three tasks—"

He was abruptly interrupted by Kate's hurtful comment: "*Woo-hoo,* Mister. You mean to tell me that you're the one behind this evil plan?" She then took a step forward and put her ear close to his chest so she could hear his heart beating. After a few moments of tense silence, she backed up a few paces and finally said, "Yup, he's human, he's got a heart." Gregorio and Ben just looked at each other, trying hard not to laugh, until it was nearly impossible. They burst out laughing. "You think this is funny? I'm just trying to be civilized here. I mean, you never know, what with the technology these days." Kate now felt embarrassed by the way she had acted. She started to laugh, too, trying to hide her shame. "You're funny, Ben. I really believed you for a second there. You scared me."

Ben now looked confused. "Wait, what are you talking about? Believe me about what?"

It was now Gregorio's turn to look stunned. "Well, about your being behind this whole evil plan, of course. It's a joke, right? Please tell me that it's just a joke."

"Oh, uh . . . no, I actually wasn't joking. I really am Ednesto's trusted advisor."

Kate was debating whether or not to check again and see if he really had a heart. It seemed as though her father had read her thoughts, because he held her back. "What do *you* have against us?" he asked the young man.

Ben seemed surprised that they were confused and so began straightening things out. "Five years ago, I had an amazing family:

two brothers, a mother, a father and a home. My parents were amazing lawyers, winning all of their cases. My brothers and I lived a luxurious life. One day, my parents got a phone call from Ednesto. He told them that he had a very important case he needed to solve and was sure that my parents would be able to help him. My parents accepted the job without even knowing the situation. They hadn't been able to refuse once Ednesto offered them a large sum of money." He now sighed, pausing briefly. "Anyway, so, once my parents became conscious of this horrible situation between the Muratis, they tried to abandon Ednesto's court case, although with Ednesto, as you might already know, there is no way out." His voice now dropped even though it retained a tone of sophistication. "I assume that you can figure out what happened next . . ." At that moment, a tear fled from the corner of his right eye.

"I'm really sorry. I didn't know. What about your brothers?" Kate asked.

Ben quickly wiped away the tear before answering. "Well, that's where I come in. You see, after Ednesto killed my parents, he wanted to make sure that anything good that my parents had owned or had created was

destroyed. As you may know already, if Ednesto
doesn't have—"

Ben was once again cut off, this time by
Gregorio, who finished his sentence. "What he
wants, no one else can have . . ."

Ben then took a few deep breaths before
continuing. "Exactly, Gregorio. I guess I'm not
the only one who knows him well, huh? Anyway,
as I was saying, he didn't want any Dingo ever
to succeed in life, and he knew that if we three
brothers are united, we can conquer anything.
So, with the help of his advisors, Ednesto
decided to separate us in different counties.
Because I'm known as the brain of the Dingo
brothers, he came to the decision that I should
be his 'trusted advisor'. He believed that he
could be a much more powerful and successful
man with my help. So, basically, that is how I
ended up here."

Kate was making dramatic sounds to
indicate her pain. With her right hand over her
heart, she began a meaningful speech about how
she completely understood Ben's life and how
hard it probably is to be him. Ben then thanked
them both for their kind words of understanding
and added one last point. "There is only one

reason why I introduced myself to you. It's to help you. Since I'm technically responsible for these unbearable tasks, I feel the urge to help. Will you let me?"

Father and daughter excused themselves and stepped aside to confer. "So, what do you think, should we trust him?" Gregorio said this quickly. It took Kate a moment to put together his words.

Speaking even more rapidly than her father, Kate replied, "Well, Ednesto is a very evil man. I would not put it past him to use this young man," she looked back at Ben, "and instruct him to lie to us. I think that this is definitely a plot. I am not getting wheeled into this one, too." Then she turned her head, showing her father that she was finished speaking. They both walked slowly towards the anxious young man, who was waiting by the boat they would soon board.

"Well, Ben, my little Katy and I have made our final decision," Gregorio stated. Kate happily nodded. Feeling certain that Ednesto was plotting against them, rejecting his plan made her feel that she had some control.

"So, Ben. Really, what we're trying to say is that we'd be thrilled if you came along with us." Kate then tried to explain that her father had made a mistake, but she was shocked to find that no sound was able to escape her lips. Instead of speaking, she grabbed her father's arm and decided to clear things up with him. "Father . . . what were you thinking?!" Even though she was angry, her father remained calm.

"Well. You know how I'm good at reading people, even if I met them just once, right?"

"Yeah, but this is Ednesto we're talking about." She was so furious that she would have railed more if her father hadn't stopped her.

"Look, sweetie, I know you're mad. I just have one simple request of you: you're going to have to trust me, okay?"

Kate was about to protest when she saw Ben come up behind her father. His face wore a large frown. Kate thought about the hardships he had already endured, and she really didn't want to cause him more pain (in the event that his story was true, not made up), so she simply answered her father kindly. "Okay, Dad, I trust you. Let's go." When Ben saw that they had both agreed to accept his help, he smirked to himself and laughed under his breath. Kate thought she heard something, but, for her father's sake, she let it slide. Once the boat was readied and they were all settled, Ben took out a map from his right pocket.

"Before I had the guts to come speak to both of you in person, I made this map. It indicates the shortest routes to your next clue for task three, so that means that it also shows you all the islands you will have to cross." Ben took a deep breath while handing over the result of his hard work to Gregorio.

"Wow, I'm impressed. Thank you so very much. We really appreciate it, don't we, Kate?" Gregorio said while alerting his daughter's foot, urging her to say something nice to reward Ben's efforts. Unfortunately, Ben saw what Gregorio was trying to do and quickly came to Kate's defense.

"Oh, it's completely fine, Mr. Tyler. By now, I understand that the preteen mind is immature." When Kate heard those words, she fumed, feeling a tremendous need to reply.

"Well, Mr. Grownup, just for your information, the last time I checked, you are a teenager yourself."

"Well, you are completely right. I might be a teenager, but at least I'm one with an active brain."

"Okay, now you have gone too far." Kate was now standing. One could feel her anger just by sitting beside her.

"Children, children, let's calm down, relax and have fun. It's a beautiful day out, and until that cruel Ednesto surprises us with his evil storm, we're safe, right?" Gregorio had spoken too soon. The moment he had uttered the word *storm,* a tremendous hurricane struck. It tipped the boat. Kate, an excellent swimmer, resurfaced after a few seconds. Once safely treading water, she looked for her father. After a few minutes, she finally saw his head, although it appeared blurry through the rain. The waves were so strong that she wasn't able to breathe properly. Every few seconds, she would find her head once again under the water. Her eyes searched and searched once more until they finally met her father's. He was standing in the middle of an island. From Kate's position, it seemed far away.

She didn't want her father to lose another of his girls, so she swam, fighting the current as hard as she possibly could. Shortly, she arrived to the island safe and sound. The moment she was on dry land, she dropped into her father's arms and passed out. Gregorio tried to revive her, but it seemed as though she had swallowed too much water. After Gregorio performed CPR on his daughter, she coughed up the water and slowly but surely rose to her feet. After an emotional scene, they both realized that Ben was missing. They yelled and shouted for a few minutes before giving up. Assuming that he was dead, they started exploring the island to find their first clue.

*   *   *

"Hey, Dad, what's for supper?" Ben asked his father while rubbing his hands.

"Well, before I tell you, I want you to tell me how your day went, Son." Ben had a charming smile on his face as he hung his jacket on the tall rack beside the door.

"Well, Dad, you know I don't have to tell you. You see everything from the—" He stopped and looked at the big screen in the middle of the dining room. "Well, the little spy camera."

Ednesto stood, showing that he was proud of his son. Putting a hand on Ben's shoulder, he replied, "I know, my child. But if it weren't for evil, where would we all be? So, tell me, Son. Tell me. I want to hear it in words, not just see it." At that very moment, Isabella walked in with a tray of hamburgers and salad.

"Before I begin, may I know who this lady is?" Ben was shocked that such a beautiful woman was their maid.

"Ah, I think it's finally time for you to meet Isabella." Ednesto lowered his voice before adding, "Our prisoner." The 19-year-old boy quickly went to help her. As he approached, he saw that her eyes were puffy and very red. He realized in how much pain she must be in at the same time he realized just how evil his father really was. "Don't help that slave," Ednesto barked. "Why do you think she's here? She's supposed to be in the dungeon. The only reason she's up here is because she kept whining about the cold down there. I mean, minus 15degrees Celsius isn't that bad, right?" He chuckled. "Anyways, so, her charge is now to be upstairs waiting on us. Leave her alone." Ben, feeling helpless, quickly obeyed his father. "So, Ben, where were we? Oh yes, you were going to tell me about your amazing day tricking the Tyler's." Ben hesitated before telling his father what had happened. He didn't like having to mention every detail when Isabella was standing nearby. Ednesto called Isabella to enter the dining room. "My son here is about to tell me how his little experience with your family went. I couldn't let you miss out on that, so, come, join us."

Isabella looked disgusted and answered him harshly. "Seeing it was enough, thank you."

Ednesto laughed to himself and then coldly replied, "The story or the dungeon?"

Chapter 8

At the very young age of 11, Kate impressed everyone with her bravery. She knew that if she believed in herself and was determined to succeed, she ultimately would succeed. Every time Kate reflected this positive attitude, she came out a winner who was able to accomplish what she wanted. This was the norm except for when Kate faced her fears.

As Kate and her father were slowly making their way across the deserted island, Kate was cautiously aware that any second, a storm or strong wind might astound them. Weather. It was one of the powers the Muratis had. A striking yet frightening bit of clout.

Now approaching a perfectly round, shiny rock, looking as though it had been scalped, Kate saw a paper beneath it. "Dad, it's exactly what Ednesto told us; the paper is under the stone. This is our next clue!" Kate was so excited that she nearly jumped. Her father, too, wore a big smile across his face. Soon, however, his smile began to fade as he tried to warn his daughter that right behind her was a mammoth wind heading in her direction—but he just couldn't speak. He felt as though he was in a daze, unable to talk, yell or even breathe. Before he knew it, he saw his daughter get caught up in the wind and fly across the island. Kate did not fear the prospect of getting hurt or falling suddenly; she was frightened about how high in the air she was. She felt as though she were flying. Really, she was flying in the midst of the whirlwind. It knew where it was supposed to go. On the other side of Windermere Lake, Ednesto stood on the balcony of an apartment he had rented for this task. He was enjoying himself like a child who had just gotten a new video game. To him, that's what this was: a game.

Kate was in the air for about three minutes. She was 80 feet off the ground and was barely able to catch her breath. As she hovered above the lake, she began to cry. Fearing for her safety, a question appeared in her mind: *Is this the end?*

Once the wind dropped her, she found herself in the lake. It was deep and the waves were choppy. Even though she was an excellent swimmer, she was having a tough time. Had it been an ordinary day, Kate would have been able to conquer this situation. But she just had suffered through her worst fear and was trembling, unable to control herself. She felt herself drowning. It was as if she saw herself in the reflection of the water, descending and making her way through the water and down to the rusty soil. She knew that these were the last seconds of her life and that neither her nor her mother had even a spark of hope of surviving.

*   *   *

"Please, no, don't kill her," Isabella said with tears in her eyes.

"Oh, Isabella, I'm not that evil, am I? It's your daughter who dragged herself into this mess, and even though you have all the power—which I will soon receive, of course—you cannot help her." He now sounded more jolly. "Well, since I am a real Murati, I was the one who inherited *The Murati Book of Spells.* No one had protested because no one believed that I was wise enough to use it. Well, they were wrong. I am wise enough to use it, and I can prove it to you. With the little power I have, I combined all three powers—of speed, fire and weather—together to create a power that prevents you from using your powers for these 11 hours."

Isabella looked annoyed and, at the same time, scared. "You think I haven't figured that out yet? Now what matters is my daughter. Please, I'll do anything—" Isabella already regretted what she had said, but it was too late.

"*Yes! Yes,* that's what I wanted to hear. Give me all your powers." Ednesto now turned away and took off his jacket as though in preparation. "Never! You know that my father would never allow this, and I won't, either. Never!"

Ednesto sat. "Well, if you find that your family power is more important than your daughter, then I guess there is nothing I can do." He now turned to face the door. He was going to leave when Isabella called out behind him.

"Yes, anything!"

*   *   *

"*Daddy!* Please help . . ." Kate was swallowing too much water and was unable to breathe. She knew that if a person couldn't get air within about two minutes, then his or her life would end. Time was running out for her; she was going to die. She thought about her friends and her mother, who was with that evil devil. She thought about her father, who was about to lose the two most important females in his life. She thought about Emily. Then she thought about her favorite teacher, Miss T, who always taught her students that everything happens for a good reason. Kate's time was now up. She was falling deeper and deeper into the lake. Suddenly, Kate was confused as her body began to rise, higher and higher. She found herself lying on hard ground, with a tall man who was holding a towel standing over her. "Where am I?" Kate managed to blurt out, her eyes still shut.

"Well, before I answer that, I demand a thank-you." Kate was about to ask who he was and why he wanted her to thank him when a familiar voice stopped her. She tried to see who it was but couldn't. The water in her eyes made it impossible for her to see the fragile daylight.

"Oh, Kate! You're alive," Gregorio said while stopping to embrace his daughter who was still lying on the ground. He then straightened up and shook Ben's wet hand. "Thank you for saving my daughter I'm really thankful. If there's anything—"

Ben lifted his hand to stop Gregorio. "Please, it's my pleasure. I understand the pain you're going through and couldn't allow you to bear more of it. This is the least I can do." Moments later, they, together with Kate, continued the journey across the dangerous island. Every step Kate and Gregorio took seemed to have been choreographed. Their fright was substantial. They had one objective, which was to cross the 18 islands safely and get to the next clue, which would lead them to their next destination.

Thirty seconds later, a big, thick, grey cloud flew above their heads, accompanied by an immense wind so strong that it blew Kate's delicate body off the ground. Once again, Ben ran to help her. As many other 11-year-old girls would do, she refused his help and was determined to do what she needed to do on her own. All of a sudden, the big cloud above their heads began increasing in size until it covered the entire island. The Tyler's automatically knew what was about to occur. Their predictions were right. Super strong rain, accompanied by lightning and thunder, started pouring down—but only on Kate and Gregorio. Ben was somehow protected by what seemed to be an invisible umbrella. Ben knew that this was his father's doing. Because he had to keep secret the fact that he was Ednesto's son, he quickly came up with an explanation for these strange circumstances. He was about to open his mouth when Kate stepped closer to him, although not too close, because she was now afraid, after having seen the strange sight. She then stretched her arm long so that it reached the space above his head. She wanted to confirm that nothing invisible was protecting him. If something was, then she would know that Ben was a wizard, just like her mother and Ednesto. She was now standing just a few inches away. Ben suddenly began to cry. Kate restrained herself, trying not to laugh. Gregorio quickly ran up to Ben, eager to discover what was wrong.

"What happened?! What's the matter?" Gregorio asked, very concerned.

"It's nothing. I'm just crying out of joy. You see, before my parents died, they told me that they would always protect me, even in minor situations. I feel that it's my parents standing over me," Ben said, feigning that he was wiping away tears. Gregorio fell for the story and began to console Ben. Kate, on the other hand, knew that it was all fakery. Something deep inside of her told her to be against Ben.

"Dad, I'm sorry to interrupt your bonding moment, but in case you haven't noticed, we're really running out of time." Ben and Gregorio brushed themselves off and followed Kate. The island was sopping wet, making it was extremely hard to walk. The sand was now mud. Kate's boots were soaked. Gregorio and Ben hadn't worn boots and were struggling in their fancy Prada shoes. Gregorio didn't want to discourage his daughter by falling to the ground. He tried very hard to remain upright, but the rain was just too strong. They were now only at the third island, with only three pieces of paper in the Tyler's' possession. They needed 15 more to complete task two. At this point, Gregorio felt that his bones had cracked. He could no longer move. Right then and there, Gregorio collapsed on the ground behind Kate and Ben. If it wouldn't have been for the loud thump of his body on the dirt, Kate would have never known that her father had fallen. She quickly turned around to find him lying there. His heart rate was diminishing by the second. Kate feared that this could be his last few moments on Earth.

* * *

Ednesto was now standing at the top of the tower in which he had rented an apartment.

His face looked very angry as he mumbled something nasty under his breath. Ben walked in abruptly. "Son, you scared me," the tall man whispered, still looking out the window and at the poor, suffering family.

"Dad, you saw me coming up," Ben said while drying the parts of his hair that had gotten wet. His father slowly turned around.

"I did not mean now, when you just entered. I meant the whole journey with the Tyler's. Why are you being pleasant, nice and kind? Son, you're a Murati, not a . . ." It seemed as though he was searching for the correct word.

Ben seemed to have found it, and then he slowly said it, only loud enough for his ears to hear: "Human." The moment he allowed that word to cross his fragile lips, he regretted it. Ben was nervous. He knew that his father would be furious. His father was now slowly approaching him.

Ednesto placed his right hand on his son's left shoulder and said, in the same volume his son just used, "Exactly."

At once, a look of anxiety crowded Ben's face. He did not know what was happening, as he had suddenly become shaken. He finally figured out what the trouble was when he saw Isabella standing right behind the door.

"Well, well, what have we got here? Has the blonde forgotten her manners? Oh, wait. The blond *has* no manners." Ednesto believed the myth that blondes were brainless. Especially now, what with Isabella's being a blonde, Ednesto had an opportunity to take advantage. His thoughts wandered until he heard Isabella abruptly answer him.

"I will have you know, Ednesto, that I was a straight-A student in all the schools I attended. The way I achieved the knowledge I have today is by practicing, which is something that a brainless person is unable to do." Isabella finished, proud of herself for answering her mean uncle that way. She hadn't, however, expected his comeback.

He laughed under his breath, ignoring her words. Before he walked away, he turned to add one more thing. "Oh, by the way, if your family continues at this rate, you can say good-bye to your life." He then looked her straight in the eye. "Unless I receive the family powers."

Very calmly, Isabella answered, "Never." But it was too late. Ednesto was already out the door. Once in his office, he looked through his papers and admired his evil plan.

*   *   *

Kate was running as quickly as she was able to. She was looking for Ben. She had been running for 25 minutes now. Still, she had been unable to locate him. When her father had fallen, he had hit his back on a sharp rock, which had made him bleed. All Kate was able to do at that moment was cover her father's wounds, desperately trying to stop the blood flow. Still, she knew that doing this would not help. Nothing would prevent her from trying to keep her father alive, however. As she resumed running through the rain, she saw lightning strike a nearby tree. She continued running. All that could be heard on that island was the sound of loud thunder and Kate's heavy breathing.

Soon, in despair, Kate sat on the ground. For an 11-year-old, she was very brave, but there is only so much drama a child can handle. Suddenly, for the first time in her life, she called out to her grandfather, desperate for help. She did not know what to say. Surprising herself, she yelled out—while looking at the sky, assuming that's where her grandfather was located—"This is all your fault. If it weren't for your reckless powers, I would be sitting happily at home with my family and friends. The least I ask from you now is to cure my father so we're able to get past this task . . . please." While Kate was skeptical that doing this would help her situation, she was hopelessly out of ideas. Within moments, she noticed a bright light shining before her. It was so blinding, that she had to turn her head completely. At first, she thought it was one of Ednesto's schemes, but when the light began to diminish, she turned to face it. She walked towards the fascinating luminosity, crossing a big puddle of mud and some broken branches. Her arm then lifted itself in the air. Kate was trying somehow to touch the light when, all of a sudden, she saw an image appear. It seemed to be the product of illusion. At a snail's pace, it started forming itself. First, Kate saw a pair of sea-blue eyes molding into a heart-shaped face, followed by a threadlike nose and, after that, thin lips. Moments later, the full face was in view. It was the figure of an old man's face, which seemed to be floating in fire. Kate opened and closed her eyes several times before determining that what stood before her was real, not an illusion. Before she was able to figure out what had just occurred, the man began to speak. His body now started to appear, forming according to his words. He began by speaking in Spanish.

Then the man said, "Kate, I am your grandfather. I heard you were in need of desperate help. What is it that you need?" His voice sounded so jolly that it put Kate on guard. She couldn't speak.

Forcing herself to make noise, Kate hollered, "What do you mean, *I heard*?" Kate made sure to emphasize the last word. She then paused dramatically before continuing. "The only reason we're in this mess is because of you, because you were unreasonable in giving all your powers to your daughter, who is right now, as we speak, locked up in a tower. But that is not the point. The point is that you caused this to come about. You don't even know how it affects us—" She was frustrated. So many nasty words, phrases and comments ran through her mind, although she wasn't able to say any of them. She wanted to, but she was simply unable. The brunette did not know what it was, but something was undeniably stopping her. Ultimately, she gave up trying and let the kind face proceed with his parley. Even though she and her grandfather were not enemies, she felt the need to call this discussion a parley.

At this point, the man's full body was visible. He was approaching Kate. The closer he got, the wider Kate's mouth grew. She could not believe her eyes as she gazed at a male version of her mother. The man before her was extremely tall; he had appeared before her in a long, shiny, gold cape over his oversized black pants. His unfortunate sense of style made Kate, (a fashion diva,) feel sorry. Kate always loved to look pretty, feeling that the way she dressed emphasized her individuality. Now, however, with her life in jeopardy, she didn't concentrate on fashion. She needed her mother, and she needed her quickly. Giving fashion tips to her grandpa was not going to save her precious mother. Instead, Kate decided to focus and begin the speech she had prepared to recite to her ancestor regarding the help she needed from him to liberate his daughter. When she was finally ready and opened her mouth, her grandfather awkwardly began humming a tune, a certain melody that sounded very familiar to

Kate. After humming, he soon began singing the words. Before Kate knew it, her grandfather was chanting. At first, Kate thought that this was a joke, but once she listened carefully, it occurred to her that the chant was the same air as her mother's music box played. Kate now dug her hand into her backpack (which she did not let go, especially after experiencing such moments in a whirlwind!) to confirm that this was the same tune as the one the man before her was singing. When she finally untangled her long fingers from her hair, she found the music box at the bottom of her backpack. As it softly played the tune she very much enjoyed hearing, Kate pulled out the music box. Now in her hand was the beautiful box playing its gorgeous melody. It seemed as if her grandfather was singing along with the descant. As he sang, Kate felt as though time had stood still. She remembered herself as an infant, listening to the song. She was going back in time. Time! She had a few hours left to complete the tasks, and yet here she was, listening to her grandfather sing. She quickly closed the music box and began to run towards her father. If her grandfather wouldn't do something about saving him, then she might as well try. She had run a few steps when she felt her grandfather's cold arm on her wrist. He quickly began speaking before she could run off.

"Kate, look around you and tell me what you see." Kate was so frustrated. She needed to find her mother. Even someone as powerful as her grandfather couldn't prevent her from doing so. She then gave her grandfather a look that meant, "Come on, Gramps. Are you serious?"

Then she tried once again to run off. This time, after he caught her, her grandfather gave her a look that said, "*It won't hurt to look once.*" For her grandfather's sake, she sacrificed a few moments and looked around. Her mouth dropped and hung open for at least 10 seconds (which, to Kate, at this point, was a lifetime). Everything in sight had frozen. Even the raindrops hovered in midair. She had come to the realization that her grandfather had frozen time. She was so amazed that she barely had the strength to get a few words out of her mouth.

When she finally collected herself, Kate smiled widely and said, "*Wow,* this is . . . wow, how'd you do this? I mean, I didn't know the Muratis had the power to freeze time. I thought you only had the power of speed, weather and fire."

There was a 20-second silence before her grandfather replied at last. In a calm and soothing tone, he said, "After a wizard like me goes to the next world, he receives double the power." He then paused, looking around at the spot where his feet stood firmly on the ground. After sighing, he picked up from where he left off. "This world," he paused, looking at his old-fashioned shoes and murmuring to himself in a near whisper. "What a world . . . what a world you live in. You know, the power to freeze time and have the whole world in your hand is the greatest feeling ever. Now, to be able to share it with you . . ." He looked up, hoping to share a sweet smile with his granddaughter. What he found instead was no response at all from Kate. It took him a few moments to realize that Kate had already run across the island in order to reach the tower and have some fun with the frozen Ednesto. The minute it occurred to the old man that his precious Kate was going to mess with his brother, he was worried. Only mortals stayed frozen when a wizard froze time. Kate's grandfather began to fret because, technically, Ednesto wasn't a human being. Therefore, he probably hadn't been frozen in time. If Kate reached the tower before her grandfather had time to stop her, she would never again see daylight. Without thinking twice, Mr. Murati, doubled his strength and doubled his speed to make it to the tower before

Kate did. He ran so swiftly that he barely noticed the ribbon fall from his braided hair. When he finally arrived, it was too late. Kate had already reached the tower and was now climbing the last step to get to her grandfather's brother's room. Even with the power of speed, he hadn't been able to outpace her. When he reached Ednesto's room, the first thing that appeared before his eyes was his granddaughter about to be cut by a knife. Mr. Murati was now certain that Ednesto hadn't frozen and was now seconds away from murdering Kate.

Chapter 9

"How did you get here, you little monster?"
Ednesto said as he held the sharp blade against
Kate's neck. He clearly wasn't aware that his
brother had descended to this world and had
frozen time to help his family. Just when Ednesto
was about to slit Kate's throat, he lifted his
dark eyes to find a pair of piercing green eyes
locking them in a stare. A sudden shock went
through him so that his now sweaty palms were
unable to hold the knife, which dropped out of
his shaking hands. It now occurred to him that
he was staring into his older brother's eyes.
Flashbacks began to rush through Ednesto's
mind. Here he was looking at the brother who
had once saved him from drowning at the
marina—the same brother who had helped
him complete his exams and the same brother
who had inherited the family burden. Ednesto
then felt a pain rush through his body—a pain
that had dwelled within him for a number of
years without exposing its source. His confused
emotions and thoughts then turned into
anger, which could become dangerous. In this
circumstance, running was Ednesto's brother's
best option. By the time Kate's grandfather had
decided to sprint in order to save himself, his

brother had already managed to lift the knife off the ground and hold it against his neck.

"Don't do this, Brother, not next to Kate," Kate's grandfather said, looking at her apologetically. That had no effect on Ednesto, however, who was a man without sympathy.

Without thinking twice, Ednesto yelled, "How many times do I have to kill you before you will leave me alone?" Ednesto was annoyed and held the knife even tighter against his brother's neck.

Then, very slowly and calmly, the old man removed the knife from his neck and, almost whispering, murmured, "Only once." Without further ado, he struck his evil brother with the knife that had once sent him to his own grave. He would now do the same to his brother. Kate fainted and fell in the blood that had poured from her great-uncle's chest. About three minutes later, she awoke with the feeling of being lofted high into the air. When her eyes opened and were able to see, she realized that she was at least four feet off the ground. It occurred to Kate that she was floating on a thick, white cloud. After Kate spent a couple of seconds processing what was happening, the cloud beneath her began letting out vapor which slowly formed into a letter. One by one, more letters appeared and began forming words. Then, the few words standing in midair turned into a sentence. "Pasa el tiempo . . . tiempo se congela . . . pero ahora, se invierte." Kate spoke very little Spanish, although she did know that that *tiempo* meant *time.* She tried to figure out the rest, but she couldn't. After a few more attempts, she began to read the words aloud. Before she knew it, she found herself in the same setting where she had been a while ago. The frozen-in-air rain surprised her again. Kate was stupefied by what the spell had done. She had gone back in time. Her grandfather was now looking at her with a proud smile on his face. Then, his smile faded as his body slowly became invisible. His features began to blur, and then he spoke with the very little breath he had left.

"My dear Kate, I descended to this world to help you, and now that I have almost completed my goal, I must leave—"

Kate didn't quite understand what was going on. With frustration and agony in her voice, she interrupted. "But, Grandfather, you haven't completed anything. My father is still lying on the ground half dead, and, evidently, I do not have the power to cure him. Please, help me."

It was now Kate's grandfather's turn to interrupt. With only a few facial features still visible, he answered. "Listen, my darling, this whole journey that we've undertaken together is just a dream. You will soon awake in the rain, at the spot where you last were crying for help. My dear Kate, I don't want you to think for one second that I am "fake". Every conversation we had was real. I came to your dream for one specific reason: to sing you the lullaby from when you were a youngster. Your mother would sing it to you every night, knowing that it would one day come in handy. That is why I am here." Her grandfather then gave her a few minutes to think over what he had just said. After crying a few tears, Kate saw that her grandfather's body was almost entirely invisible and demanded that he begin to sing the song before he completely disappeared. Before he commenced, he added something to calm her. "Kate, I just want to tell you that you should not be worried about time, since you were only sleeping for 36 seconds, so—" He was then once again interrupted, although this time for the good.

"Listen, I know you care for me, but my pressing concern is the amount of time you have. So, please hurry and sing the song. Complete your mission," Kate said. Her grandfather then slowly lowered his head as though agreeing with what she had just said and subsequently he began singing the traditional family song.

When it's hard, when life seems to turn its back, don't give up. Just continue and turn to the right, and remember not to let go of the sack. Jump three times, like you're flying a kite, and then close your eyes, as though you're in a windy desert. Then, roll on the ground for a better view of the stars. After that, slowly get up and button your coat so you don't get hurt. Then, run to left, and live your life as passing cars. And remember, it's not the load that breaks you; it's the way you carry it.

When Kate's grandfather ended the song, he told her that he had to leave and that it was time for her to leave, as well. She refused to let him go until he agreed to explain the significance of the song. "Please, Grandfather, tell me the meaning. I know you know. After all, you wrote it."

Her grandfather was now seconds from disappearing. He answered her. "On the 13th birthday of a male Murati who was born and brought down to this world, he receives a vision of one of his children or grandchildren in pain, and through that vision he creates something to guide him or her through the difficulty. Whenever you sing this song, remember to add 'for my' at the end—" Before he was able to finish his sentence, he vanished. Moments later, Kate was lying on the cold, muddy ground and realized that she had awakened from her dream and was now facing reality. Before Kate went to look for her father, she quickly dug her hand into her backpack and took out her fluffy pink pen and shiny notepad. She then rapidly wrote down the words to the song. Given her inadequate short-term memory, at a time like this, she would never remember the lyrics.

Somehow, she knew that this song was very important. If she wanted to get through the difficulty she was currently facing, she would—by hook or by crook—need the lullaby. As she wrote the last few words, she realized that her grandfather had not completed the song and that if she needed to sing it to get herself out of a jam, she would not be able to access its full potential. She put that thought aside for now and instead focused on the matter of finding her father and completing task two. Before she was able to look around for her father, she saw Ben coming towards her, wearing an anxious frown on his face. Since Kate had first met that young man, she was suspicious of him. She never liked him. Before Ben reached her, she asked, "So, what's the matter this time?" Ben frowned more deeply, putting a hand to his face, and forced a tear to roll down his left cheek. Kate intuited that this was melodrama and concluded that Ben was bluffing. Without further ado, Kate and him went to go find her father. At that moment, Ben collected himself, realizing that Kate had seen through his countenance of mock sorrow. He walked over to her.

"Okay, listen, Ben. I don't know about you, but I am going through a really hard time. Unless you tell me what your desire is, I'm afraid that I cannot help you," Kate said in a rush. She then turned away, desperate to search for her father.

Ben hesitated and then answered. "All I want—" He paused dramatically. "All I want is to help you." Kate was annoyed and didn't have the patience to answer. She began walking away, and Ben followed. She let him tag along. Of course, this meant that she would listen to several of his comments that she'd rather not hear. Kate noted that Ben was just like the boys she knew at school. They were immature but sometimes put on an air of maturity in an attempt to present a false image of themselves. Since Kate knew boys, she knew exactly how to act with Ben. Just when Kate was about to reply to his *latest* annoying comment, she caught a glimpse of a healthy man running around and looking lost. Being that Kate was a compassionate and caring person, she couldn't help but go and find out if he needed any help. When she and Ben were close enough to the man to identify him, Kate realized that it was her father. She was surprised to see him behaving this way. He was always poised and calm, but not now, especially after his incident. His running around was strange. Kate wished to attribute his behavior to too much coffee, but he had his coffee hours ago. She slowly approached him, her hands firmly behind her back.

At the present moment, Kate was terribly afraid that her father might be sick. That would add to her already full cup. Without further ado, she addressed him. "Daddy, is everything okay? You're looking kind of . . . out of place." Kate paused a few moments, grabbing a water bottle from her backpack. She quickly handed it to her father, sure that his problem was thirst. She reassured him that it would make him feel better. Normally, Gregorio would gulp down the drink, since water was, after all, his favorite. Instead, Gregorio calmly placed the water bottle on the ground, looked at the frightened Kate and Ben, and repeated his foolish behavior. Unable to restrain himself, Ben laughed at 'his uncle's' unwise behavior. Kate, too, thought it was funny, although she understood that it was truly inappropriate to laugh at such a moment. Ben told Kate that if they waited a few minutes, her father would return to normal. They both tried to convince themselves that he just needed to let everything out—that he missed his beloved wife and feared losing her. The two of them watched for about seven minutes until they realized that something was terribly wrong. Ben decided that it would be a good idea to approach him. Gregorio and Ben had bonded when they first met, and this is what compelled Ben to help now. Even though Kate was initially hesitant, ultimately she had to agree to Ben's plan, seeing as no one else was there for backup. The only difficulty was getting Gregorio to listen. They tried attracting him, but each time he saw them, he looked anxious and ran away. Then, the brilliant Kate came up with a plan.

All members of the Tyler family were musicians who were fascinated by music. Therefore, Kate's idea was to make music with anything she was able to find on the deserted islands in Windermere Lake. Once she found her 'instruments,' she and Ben would begin making music. As soon as Gregorio noticed it, he would surely approach and attempt to locate its source. Then, he would be close enough to Ben and Kate, who might be able to find out what was troubling Gregorio. Furthermore, if Gregorio decided to run away, Ben would tie his hands together and get to the bottom of things!

Kate and Ben were now in position to 'capture' Gregorio. All went as planned. Gregorio followed the music, dancing a little along the way, yearning to see where the sound was coming from. When he found the source, he was startled to learn that he had been tricked and attempted to run, but it was too late. His hands were already tightly tied behind his back by a long, strong, uncomfortable leaf. Kate was about to begin speaking when her father abruptly shouted, "What is it that you want from me? I have no money, no gold! Find someone else to rob!"

Confused, Kate approached her father, giving him her hand while pleading, "Please, Daddy, I don't like this game. Stop, please!"

Looking at her hand, her father answered in a near whisper. "'Daddy'? I was never married. I never had a daughter. Who are you?"

Chapter 10

❧ • ❧

Upon hearing her father's few words, Kate froze, staring straight into his eyes. She knew that something was wrong, but what could it be? Why would her father act this way? She pretended that she had not heard her father's words and tried to put on a smile. Ben, on the other hand, reacted differently. Worried, he took Kate aside, asking her if this had ever happened before. With tears in her eyes, she shook her head slightly and then ran over to her father, who was staring at the both of them with deep confusion in his eyes. Aware that time was a precious gem, Kate had no time to cry; instead, she was absolutely determined to discover what her father's problem was. She slowly approached him, deep in concentration, searching for the words to say. When she was finally a hairsbreadth away from her father, she whispered loud enough for Ben, who was just feet away, to hear.

"Father, I don't know what is going on, but I would just like to say that you are married and you do have a child—" She hesitated, backing away a few feet so he could see her clearly. In a louder, more powerful voice, and while tearing up a bit, Kate said, "I am your child, Father. It's

me, Kate, your firstborn. Please . . . remember."
The young girl then sat on the ground and
buried her head deep in her hands. Then her
head abruptly shot up. "Remember," she slowly
whispered. She then ran to her confused father,
as if something had caught her eye. The back
of her father's head was cut and ejecting blood.
She quickly took off her cardigan, dipped it in
water and gently wrapped it around her father's
head. She looked around the small island to find
where he had hit his head. Five feet away from
them was a sharp rock covered with blood.
The 11-year-old was about to cry, but then her
facial expression transformed. She smiled. She
had finally learned the reason for her father's
strange behavior. He had amnesia!

Ben was relieved and also felt happy for
a few moments, until he realized that Kate was
staring at his watch, trying to make out the time.
Ben deliberately put on a serious expression and
delicately sat in front of 'his uncle.'

"In school, I was taught that when a
person has amnesia, he does not remember daily
things, for example, his family, his friends, his
job." Ben paused, wearing a deep frown. Facing
Kate, he continued. "It's sad, but, sometimes,
the person doesn't remember his name—"

Hearing a loud gasp, Ben paused for a few moments, giving Kate some time to comprehend the information he had just imparted. After a minute, Ben continued, this time with a firm tone of voice. "The complex fact about amnesia is that the sufferer does not remember 'daily life information.' The person lives in the past, meaning that he only remembers his childhood. It's multifaceted. A person with amnesia is even able to remember songs from when he was a toddler."

Satisfied that he had filled Kate's ears with the information she needed to know, the 17-year-old turned his body to face Gregorio, who was tied to a tree. When he was about to open his mouth and find out at what stage of his life Gregorio was 'in' at this point, Ben was surprised to find Gregorio going through his pockets, repeating that he needed to find his map. Politely, Ben approached him. "Mr. Tyler," he said. Gregorio looked up slightly as the son of Ednesto cleared his throat. "Hi. I was walking on this beautiful island and happened to notice that you were looking for something, is there anything I can help you with?"

Abruptly, Gregorio lifted his head, as if forgetting he was attached to a tree. With a kind, friendly smile, he introduced himself. "Hey, I'm Greg. Nice to meet you." Kate's father then paused and turned his gaze to his daughter. Slightly nodding, he continued. "As I was saying, I don't know how I arrived here. All I know is that I really need to find my map. The thing is, I'm planning my friend's party, and I need to call the caterer to confirm the cake and—" Gregorio was interrupted by Kate's sudden outburst.

"I'm sorry to interrupt you," Kate began, sounding uncomfortable as she approached her father. The young girl took a few moments to look at her father and make sure it was him. She was uncertain, given his last few words. "I'm still stuck on your last few words. Am I correct? I heard you say 'party.' I am puzzled."

Gregorio, appearing a little puzzled himself after Kate's curious question, tried to take a step forward. Now, he realized that he was tied to the tree. Shrugging his shoulders and appearing not to care, he hesitantly spoke to the young girl before him. "I guess I have just come to the understanding that I am no in the year 1990?! Going back in time is weird!" Upon seeing Kate's terrified expression, Gregorio interrupted himself. With mixed feelings, he decided to say something to erase what he had just said, thinking that that must be the problem. A few silent moments passed. The only sound was from glad birds chirping in the treetops. Gregorio's deep voice broke the silence. "Hey, I'm really sorry. I didn't mean to shock you. It's just I've never traveled back in time, and I find that it's kind of bizarre. Wait . . . who are you?"

Kate sighed slowly and deeply as she watched her father's disease grow worse every second. "Oh, I hope this is temporary," Kate cried, looking up at the sky.

"I sure hope so, too," Gregorio whispered in her ear behind her. Kate, unaware that Ben had taken pity on her father and untied him, was startled. "I mean, I really need to get to that sweet 16, particularly because I'm the one planning it."

Tears began to fill up the young girl's eyes. She tried to hold them back, but it was nearly impossible to stop them from streaming down her warm cheeks. Forgetful Gregorio sat beside her, asking who she was and why she was crying. Unable to bear the pain, Kate got up and ran towards Ben. He was sitting in a little corner of the island on the trunk of a tree. It was so big it seemed to be a bench. The young man seemed deep in thought when Kate disturbed him with her own thoughts. Kate was about to throw all of her anger at Ben because he hadn't helped when he motioned for her to take a seat beside him. Calming her temper, Kate sat down and took a long, deep breath. Ben started speaking. Once he did, Kate began to relax. She wasn't sure if it was his pure voice or his soothing words. Which ever it was, she was just happy that she was able to escape from the world for a few moments and just concentrate on the beautiful stories and expressions Ben told her, which sent a feeling of tranquility through her stiff body. After a while, Ben stopped, leaving pleasant thoughts wandering through Kate's mind. "Listen, Ben, as annoying as you may be and as weird as it is to talk to you, I just want you to know that you lightened my spirits in a time of need. I truly have to thank you for that." Ben's reply was to slightly nod his head and smile delicately. Then, as though hesitant to tell him something, Kate blurted, "Seeing you in your present state with no parents, because of that evil Ednesto." She mumbled the last few words under her breath and was about to continue when, seeing Ben flush, she stopped herself and tried to think of something to say to erase the effect of her blunt comment. What Kate didn't know was that Ben's thoughts were radically different from hers.

Now that he was building a friendship with Kate, Ben felt that it was wrong that she should still believe his lie. He felt that as a friend whom Kate trusts for the time being, he should tell her the truth about who his father really is. It was at this time that Ben decided to confide in her.

"I have something really important to tell you," Ben began while rubbing his sweaty palms.

Curious, Kate whispered, "Go ahead."

Here it goes, Ben thought to himself as if boarding a car on a long roller coaster. "About my 'dead' parents, I—" At that moment, they heard a loud splash. Both Kate and Ben stood, frightened. Ben was about to finish his sentence when he noticed that Kate had already run over to discover the source of the sound. He followed her to a spot just a few yards away from where he had been sitting a few minutes earlier. Once near Kate, Ben's eyes widened in surprise. His mouth dropped in response to what was before him.

"How did this happen?" Kate asked Ben, not wanting an answer. The boy was so shocked by the sight that, even if he wanted to answer, he wouldn't be able to.

*   *   *

"Oh, how much I missed you!" Ednesto said to the young woman standing in front him. Dressed in a black pencil skirt, she straightened out her striped shirt that was neatly positioned beneath her Gucci blazer.

After having advanced towards him, she slowly said to him. "It's always a pleasure to be back." She then turned away, concentrating on her open suitcase. After a few long moments, she turned around and, smiling broadly, said in a jolly tone, "Who else would do all the work for you?" As Ednesto was about to reply, he saw his son walk in. Soon enough, his words faded and never crossed his lips.

"Ben, what a surprise. Aren't you supposed to be down there?" Ednesto said, pointing at the islands below and giving a quick wink.

"Well, I thought I'd take a break." Ben paused to hang his damp jacket on the nearby rack. As he rubbed his feet against the reflective carpet, he continued. "Plus, I'm famished. The air out there is really humid, and—" Ben stopped as he noticed the young woman standing before him. Soon enough, he ran over to hug her.

"Mom, when did you arrive? I missed you!"

At 40 years old, Ben's mom was still beautiful. Ben slowly approached the large window standing opposite the dining room and looked through it, as though making sure that the Tyler's were okay. They had just made it to the 13th island. He smiled, happy for them, and quickly did the math. "Five more islands and one more task, with three and a half hours left. That'll do." He felt relieved and let out a large sigh, then felt his father's big palm resting on his left shoulder. Ben quickly turned around and grinned.

"What is it that made you look out that window, Son? Is there something wrong?"

Speechless, all Ben could do was look down at his watch and pretend that he hadn't heard his father question. Soon enough, he felt his father's gaze on him and lifted his head to find his father giving him a mocking glance and motioning for him to speak up. A few long moments passed. The atmosphere became thick and awkward. Ben's mother broke the silence by suggesting that they all sit. Ednesto hesitated, desperately wanting to learn why his son appeared so bold. *Why is he acting this way? Is he not on my side?* thought Ednesto. As delicious-smelling food was placed before them, all three quickly took their seats. Their mouths were watering. Ednesto was eager to find out why his son was so involved with the Tyler's. As he began again to ask Ben, he saw mother and son exchange a knowing glance. The words died on Ednesto's lips as he felt a certain feeling overcome him, one he had never felt before. He felt regret.

Chapter 11

"My, it's getting hot out here," Kate said while wiping her forehead. As she allowed her eyes to linger on the beautiful islands, she watched the lake as its waters swayed slowly from side to side, as oppose to minutes earlier when her father attempted to swim. Little did he know that Windermere is not a swimming place. Thinking back at those moments sends shivers down her spine as she continues looking at the island until she catches sight of her father trying to figure out a way out of the island, with the help of his map. "If I turn right . . . . maybe left . . ." He was cut short by his daughter's soft weeping. As he looked up with a guilty smile, he saw Kate. She looked flushed. Gregorio didn't know that she desperately wanted to get to the last island, receive her final task and then, soon afterwards, find her mother. Knowing nothing of Kate since his 'accident,' he hurried towards her in sympathy, as if he knew all about her family background.

As her 'teenager' father approached, Kate began to have mixed feelings about her current situation. She felt terror and fright slide across her spine once she glanced up to find her father approaching her, smiling a jolly smile. She was no longer able to control herself. She began to yell at her so-called father. "Don't you comprehend? I cannot believe how ignorant a person can be." She paused a moment, clutching her bag tightly against her chest. Moments passed as her anger filled the air. The atmosphere was dense with rage, thick as if a bomb had just detonated, its smoke now dispersing in the air. As Kate began to move towards her father with a frustrated look in her eyes, she let out a piercing screech that, she was sure, reached all the way to Buckingham Palace. She screeched for about seven seconds, but it echoed for a long while. Moments later, when the uncomfortable sound began to fade, Kate silently took her seat on one of the tall trunks beside her. She sat cross-legged, feeling that for task two, she would have to do something truly unpleasant.

*   *   *

As she sat in the dark, Isabella was convinced that she would be safe. She had no doubt that her beloved family would succeed in their mission, but her stomach was uneasy nonetheless. She hadn't eaten any decent food in nearly two full days. Her skeletal body reflected how she was feeling inside. As she slowly bent her head, she reached into her pocket. As she searched inside, she felt the edge of her finger touch a wrinkled piece of paper. Once she brought out the paper, she flashed back to when she had first written on it.

> Dearest Kate,
> You are now 11 years old. You're beautiful and talented and, of course, the best daughter anyone could ask for. As I write this letter to you, I want you to remember that wherever life takes you, I will always be here for you. As evidence of my love and loyalty, I entrust to you this ring that has been in our family for over 500 years.

Isabella stopped reading and once again put her hand in her dress pocket. She slowly pulled out a tiny object. It was a beautiful ring made of white gold. It lit the whole dungeon. As she let the ring roll in her cold, pale palm, she continued to read.

And I hope that you will treasure and love it as much as I treasure and love you.

Happy birthday, sweetie!

Love,

Mom

"If only I could give it to her!" Isabella said in a near whisper as she folded the wrinkled paper and put the precious ring inside, making sure that there was no way for it to fall out. To do this, she made a small hole at the top of the paper, took the ribbon from her long, blonde hair, which gracefully brushed her shoulder, and rolled the ring towards the middle of the ribbon while tying its two ends together through the small hole she had made moments earlier. When the ring was safe inside, Isabella folded the letter one more time. The beautiful blonde then stared at the tiny parcel for a few moments. Suddenly, a shadow fell across the worn-out paper. Before she had a chance to look up, she heard Ednesto's aggressive breathing.

"My, my, what have we got here?" He paused as he examined from afar the paper Isabella was holding. He continued. "It is against

111

the law to let prisoners have their own diaries. Prisoners—" he paused, after emphasizing the *P*, "have no right to own anything, except, of course, their worthless garments." Ednesto then stopped making it obvious that he had nothing to say. He waited a few moments for Isabella to answer, but the only sounds he heard were the tiny footsteps of the creepy-crawlies nearby. Angered that his niece didn't answer, Ednesto tried to provoke her a second time. To Ednesto, it seemed that Isabella didn't answer because she wanted to frustrate him. But the real reason for her unusual silence was her lack of energy. She was so out of, well, *everything*, which made it impossible for her to speak. "As I was saying," Ednesto continued, hoping to erase the embarrassing moment when he had nothing to say. He paused dramatically, examining his niece for a few moments as he paced back and forth along the old and dirty wood floor beneath his feet. Soon enough, a small smile appeared on his dark face. It was a smile that seemed to indicate that he had found what he was looking for. Indeed, he had. "Listen, Isabella. Just because you're my niece doesn't give you the right to do whatever you want, okay?" Ednesto said, approaching Isabella. Isabella was so tired that she just wanted him out of 'her room.' She needed some time to be alone and spill her feelings, even in that spooky dungeon.

Without further ado, Isabella slowly answered, almost in a whisper. "Ednesto, please. I don't understand. What do you mean, 'do whatever I want'? I'm the most obedient captive in this solemn dungeon," she said, pointing to other prisoners locked behind bars. *Poor them* she thought to herself, the same way Ednesto had a dungeon back home, he had one here too, and one in almost every country as well. As she inhaled deeply to muster the strength to continue, the young mother was soon interrupted by her evil uncle.

"Hmm. There's no need for them to be obedient. They're all dead!" The air became thick, falling on Isabella as her uncle's words sunk into her ears. She interrupted him. "As I mentioned previously, I don't see how I am 'doing whatever I want.' So, please, Ednesto just—"

"Well, well, with what little energy you have, I wouldn't have expected to hear from your big mouth. If you insist on knowing, the reason I said 'do whatever you want' is simply because you are leaving your hair down."

"Excuse me? I'm sorry. I'm not sure I heard you correctly. You're yelling at me for letting my hair down? Clearly, there is something wrong with—" Isabella said with a sudden energy that overpowered her, then stopped mid-sentence as she felt someone pulling her hair. The pain was so terrible that she couldn't utter a single word through her thin lips. It felt as though someone had gripped her hair tightly, as if it were a bundle of wheat. Sensing a bit of strength, turned her head to see what was going on with her hair. Upon beholding what lay behind her, she let out a screech so loud that it threatened to wake the nearby dead. It was a big, hairy man, wearing a burgundy sash over his green military-style suit. In his oversized hand was a fat, grey, old-fashioned shaver, which he placed against Isabella's beautiful curls.

"*No*, please, it's my only . . . enjoyment. I—"

"Enough with the drama, you," the man said. Then, he abruptly stopped, as though listening to something far away. He smiled gently.

"My only enjoyment?" Ednesto said, perfect mimicking Isabella. "It's amazing how you're able to enjoy stuff, knowing that you're dying in just a few hours. I'm impressed. It's—"

"That's enough!" Isabella yelled to her uncle, gathering her strength to get to her feet. Still holding Kate's gift, she continued. "Please. Every human being has bit of good in them. I don't believe that even the meanest, most cruel being can be fully bad. Please, just—" Isabella slowly made her way towards her uncle, hoping to make him realize that what he was doing was inhumane and attempting to evoke his sympathy by stressing that she was family to him. When she was a few centimeters away from Ednesto, she felt the atmosphere soften. For the first time, she was sure that Ednesto had listened to her pleas. A thin smile began to appear on his face, perfectly settling under his dark mustache. Isabella shed a tear of joy, feeling that this was all over, certain that Ednesto was finally able to understand the most important concept in the world: family. As she approached him, she flashed her million-dollar smile. She was finally happy. If she had known what was to occur shortly thereafter, she never would have had these feelings about her uncle.

In the next few moments, all the happiness and joy Isabella had just experienced was shattered. A pair of sweaty hands clutched her hair and pulled it so tight that it felt like a fan sucking her hair into its blades. What awaited her, though, was much worse.

"To think that I trusted you, you—"

"Oh, that's enough of you and your whining. You know what, Isabella? I'll make a deal with you. You stop whining and engaging in drama, and I'll let you keep one strand of your hair. How about that?" Ednesto said with an evil smirk. Isabella responded with absolute silence. The silence didn't last long, however. Once the man in the green military suit and a burgundy sash replaced the fat, grey razor with a knife the size of Isabella's arm, Isabella went from silence to sobbing. Rango, his name was, started cutting her beautiful golden curls. Of course, he made sure to take his time. Following Ednesto's orders, he slashed off Isabella's hair, making sure that she felt pain. Ednesto issued a barrage of cruel comments, mentioning that Isabella would soon die and that life for her was now worthless. But despite Ednesto's words, Isabella *fully* believed that her life was precious, even though something deep inside was telling her that her family wasn't going to succeed. She knew that, no matter what, her life was precious and—

Her thoughts were suddenly interrupted by something horrendous, an unbearable sight. She found herself looking at her reflection in a shiny mirror held by two scary-looking men who resembled Rango. The mirror looked as though it had been polished especially for her, to make sure that she could see every detail. The beautiful Isabella was now seeing something that was definitely *not* beautiful. Her gorgeous, long blond curls were all gone; she had short hair, so short that it barely reached her shoulders. She turned, enraged. She was surprised to find Rango and Ednesto engaged in a little chat while Rango emptied the razor he had used just moments before on the poor Isabella. Once gathering her strength, Isabella stood and cried to her uncle so loudly that the guards were shocked. As she bawled, Ednesto just looked at her with an evil smile. When Isabella's strength was gone and she was forced to stop shouting, Ednesto gracefully advanced towards her with a pitying look on his face. He gently removed the note addressed to Kate from Isabella's soft hand and placed it in his pocket.

The letter was gone.

The ring was gone.

Was the life Isabella had dreamed of, the one she lived with Kate and Gregorio, over?

Chapter 12

The unbearably hot sun was still, shining above the beautiful islands in Windermere Lake. As Kate and her 'father' searched for the note under a rock which beneath a tree, she felt the sun burning her face.

"Weather. This has to be about one of the three powers the Muratis possess. I mean, it couldn't be . . . invisibility, could it? How cool would that be, huh? Da—" Kate turned around to find her father rolling up his sleeves, hoping to cool down but still making sure that he was 'in style.' She stopped speaking and shed a tear. Poor Kate now felt abandoned. She had no father to help her fight for her mother's life. In fact, she had absolutely no one to help her get through this hard time. As she tried to reflect on something positive, something that would motivate her to continue, she heard her father, behind her, let out a huge sigh. As turned to look at him, she saw him walking slowly towards her with a confused look on his face. *Not again,* Kate thought to herself.

When Gregorio was a few feet in front of his daughter, he slowly asked, "Where am—"

Kate interrupted his sentence. She had heard it too many times and didn't want hear it again, what with only three hours and a half left. She couldn't afford to lose even one second, so, surprising her father, she answered each one of the questions he hadn't asked yet. By now, Kate knew them by heart, because of the other 13 times he had asked.

Stunned, her father blurted out, "Are you a mind reader?" To have some fun, Kate decided to tell him that she was. Kate would describe the look that appeared on her father's face as priceless. Even though she knew that her father was unaware of everything going on in her life, she felt like spilling her feelings. Since he was the only one around to talk to, Kate kept the conversation going. As she was speaking to her father, he pushed her and threw her on the ground. Angered, she turned around again to find her father hiding behind a tree. Kate was shocked, but not at the sight of her father. What shocked her was the huge hurricane she saw coming their way. Kate hurriedly ran towards the tree her father was hiding behind. To Gregorio, it felt as if the hurricane was following them. Kate knew that Ednesto had programmed the hurricane to regard her and her father as the target. That's how things stood for a few minutes, although, to Kate and her father, it felt like hours. Everywhere they ran, the hurricane chased them. Ednesto had sent the hurricane because he wanted to watch Kate and Gregorio, depleted of strength, give up.

After three more minutes of running, father and daughter sat down on the ground beside a tree. As Kate lifted her arms in desperation, she heard herself whisper slowly, "I can't take this any longer! I give up." Soon, the hurricane began disappearing in midair.

"Finally, that thing is gone. But it's boiling out here. At least this refreshed us" Gregorio said as he looked down at his drenched clothing. "Its crazy how with the little magic he has he is capable of performing such things, it's agonizing."

"Who's Ednesto? You keep repeating that name, although you've never actually told me about him," Gregorio said.

Kate was about to begin patiently explaining to her father, for the 10th time, who Ednesto was. Just then, a gigantic cloud appeared above the Tyler's' heads. Within seconds, it began to rain. These were no ordinary raindrops, however. Each was at least three inches larger than the usual raindrop, which might have not made a difference if it was only drizzling. But this was a rainstorm. In addition, drops fell in bundles of 20 so that, once they hit a person's body, they really stung. For 10 minutes, as Kate and Gregorio walked the island searching for the clue, the only sound came from Kate was, "Ouch, ouch, ouch."

"How is it possible that I am the one who can wish for something and then receive it? I mean, it's not like there is someone mean up in the sky who exists only to harm us, listening to every word we say so as to grant our wishes in ways that make things worse." For the first time since he had hit his head, Gregorio seemed to know exactly what was going on.

Kate's response was to say, "Exactly." As she and her father continued their journey on island number 15, Kate caught sight of a little piece of paper under a tiny rock. It was soaked. She quickly bent down and grabbed the little piece of paper, holding it tightly between her fingers for a few moments before opening it to find her next riddle. Prior to this time, Gregorio had solved each riddle for most of the islands. Now, however, her father was mentally unavailable. She was afraid of the riddle she would find on the paper. She took a few seconds to catch her breath before unfolding the note. Reassuring herself that she'd be able to discover the answer, she read it aloud: "I'm a psychological time machine. I occur if a man hits his head on . . . ?"

Kate slowly folded the paper and placed it on the muddy ground in front of her feet. She then sat down next to it, indifferent to the mud. Placing her hands on her head, and deep in concentration, she reread the letter until she felt her father's breath on her right shoulder. She turned her head to find him deep in concentration, as well, trying to figure out the answer to the riddle.

"This is hopeless," Kate said as she repositioned herself on the dirt. "Oh, don't say that. You're always so hard on yourself. I may not know you, but you seem to be a very bright girl. I'm sure that if we brainstorm, we'll figure it out together and get the answer to lead us to the next island. I guess we should just take it one step at a time." As Gregorio continued talking, Kate felt that her father had returned to his right mind. She was glad that, at least, she had him. Searching for her mother made her realize the value of family, how important everything in life was, and that she should appreciate everything. Of course, she should also thank G-d for every little thing she had.

"So, Kate, let's do this." Gregorio gently placed his hand on the piece of paper and lifted it, holding it at each corner to make sure it wouldn't fall apart, given the rain and the mud. Then, he reread the riddle, hoping eventually to determine the answer. "So, a psychological time machine. *Psychological* means 'in the brain,' which means that this is something one cannot see. And a time machine. Well, a time machine transports people through time, so—" Gregorio stopped in mid-sentence because he heard Kate murmur something. He tried to make out the words spoken in a voice too soft to hear above the noise of the cloudburst. Soon, Kate repeated what she had said. Once again, Gregorio wasn't able to hear her. Gregorio approached Kate and kindly asked her to repeat what she had said. As quietly as before, she said it again.

"Amnico," she said.

"Am what?"

"Amnico. It's a type of disease that is a psychological time machine. It's like amnesia, except . . . it's a little different. It's—"

Kate's father interrupted her. It was hard to tell if Gregorio was surprised or confused. "Wait, how do you know all this information? I thought you were only 11." After a few long moments of silence, Kate finally answered her father.

"Well," she began dramatically, "it happens to be that someone in my family actually has this disease, which is how I know about it. Never mind that, though. Let's continue."

"Oh, I'm so sorry. Um, who in your family was diagnosed with it?" Silence filled the air. Every moment that passed brought thicker tension. Gregorio broke the silence. "You know what? It doesn't matter. Let's continue. So, did you figure out the cause of it, if a man hits his head on . . . ?"

As Kate furtively wiped away a tear, she turned to her father with puffy eyes. Pretending not to notice, Gregorio anxiously awaited her answer. Kate whispered, "A sharp rock. If a man hits his head on a sharp rock."

At this point, Gregorio had once again forgotten where he was standing. One thing, however, was for sure: anyone standing in his shoes would be able to sense this young girl's pain and agony. This time, unlike the other 10 times, Gregorio did not ask any questions. He just followed Kate and made a commitment to himself to support her during what seemed to him to be a hard time.

Once Kate had solved the riddle, she let her eyes wander around and look for the island with the sharp rocks. Soon enough, she found it. As Kate motioned for Gregorio to sit in a canoe, she explained to him that they would be heading to another island where they would hopefully find another small piece of paper, which would lead them to yet another island. Pretending that he knew what was going on, Gregorio nodded and repeated "Everything will be fine" so many times that he finally forgot why he was saying it.

Father and daughter were rowing close to the shore and towards their next island, one full of pointy rocks. The rain was coming down so hard that when it hit a rock, the water bounced off its surface. As the canoe approached the island, Kate began to make out a figure, someone dressed in black. She wasn't sure who it was. Hoping to find out, she began to accelerate. She paddled so fast that, once she reached the island, her arms hurt and she was barely able to move them. Once she got out of the canoe, she approached the man. It was Ben.

"So, how's your journey so far?" Ben asked, concerned.

"Well, let's see: a father with amnico, a missing mother, a crazy great-uncle, and no help at all. You decide how you want to put it."

"Oh, come on. Don't be that way. Look at the positive side." He paused to look at Kate and found her staring back at him with a curious smirk on her face. "Well," he resumed, turning as though leading the way, "you have me, who's pretty helpful. Aren't I?"

"Of course you are."

Kate then stopped in her tracks as an idea occurred to her. "Since you're the mastermind behind all this, and since you're trying to be helpful and show that you care, how about you find us our next letter, our next clue?"

It was now Ben's turn to stop and turn towards Kate. He slowly advanced in her direction. Almost whispering, he said, "I've got something even better for you." Curious, Kate demanded to know what he was talking about. Ben inserted his hand into his right pocket and discreetly produced a piece of paper. It was Isabella's letter.

Chapter 13

"What is this?" Kate asked, hearing her father's footsteps approaching from behind. Waiting for an answer, Kate noticed Ben look from side to side as if checking to see if the coast was clear. Then, he began explaining.

*   *   *

In the corner of the room, Ednesto sat by his desk and examined a map. It was strange, a map like no other. With the little tracking dot that moved across the map in conjunction with the Tyler's' movements, Ednesto knew exactly where they were. He heard the front door open and saw his son enter the room. Hurriedly placing the map on the nearest table, Ednesto, smiling contentedly, approached his son.

"Son," Ednesto said as he stood from his big leather armchair. Straightening his cape, he continued. "Good to see you. You'll never believe what I did today," he said, forcing another smile.

"What now, Dad? What is the *awesome* thing you've done now?" Surprised by his son's tone of voice, Ednesto approached him and looked him straight in the eye. "Benjamin, what is this strange behavior of yours? Lately, I noticed that you're acting very strange, as if you're . . . attached to this family. I'm hurt, Son. What has happened?"

Afraid, Ben didn't feel able to tell his father the truth. How could he possibly tell his father that he knew that he was evil? How could Ben disappoint his father and let him know that he had become attached to the Tyler family? He decided to keep playing along, especially since he needed information from his father to help the Tyler's and save them from tragedy. "Well, Dad, you know, the Tyler's are a big pain and I'm sick of them. I guess that's why I'm acting this way."

A long silence fell upon them. Ednesto remained unconvinced after his son's hesitant explanation. He said, "Uh-huh."

Wanting to get information out of his father, Ben leisurely asked him what he had wanted to ask moments earlier. Unconvinced that his son was telling the truth, Ednesto only gave Ben part of the story. "Well, Benjamin, if you must know, then I will tell you only part of it, since I'm still unconvinced that you're on my side, if you know what I mean. So, all I will say is this." As Ednesto sat and began telling the story, his son, sitting beside him, listened in fascination. Ednesto provided many details about the previous scene with Isabella. Nearing the end of his story, Ednesto spoke more slowly. Ben knew that there was a lot more to the end. As he sat in suspense before his father, he listened in awe. Then, his father came to an abrupt halt. Ben felt that he had been denied the chance to learn what happens at the end of this fairy tale—which, he hoped, would include, "And they lived happily ever after."

"Wait!" Ben called out. His father turned his head away, making it clear that he was finished telling his story. "Please. What happened after that, after the part when you noticed the paper in her hand? Did you take it? What did you do? Please, tell—"

"That's enough, Son. I already told you that I am not fully convinced of your loyalty. You should at least be thankful that I filled you in on the majority of the story."

"But—" Ben tried to insist, but after a while, he found himself in the room alone and realized that he was talking to a wall. Soon enough, he gave up. On his way to leave the room, something strange caught his eye. He drew near to the object, which seemed out of place. As he slowly approached it, he felt a shadow fall across him. The object was engulfed in the shadow, too. Not turning to see who was standing behind him, he quickly rushed towards the object to determine what it was. Once he had made out its shape, he suddenly became frightened. It was a gloved hand, visible for only a few seconds, although somehow the shadow remained for a much longer time. As Ben stood there facing the place where he had first seen the object, he felt the air thickening and was afraid. The atmosphere felt strange. Ben was sure that if anyone walked in, they would run straight out of the room because of the friction and tension. Gradually, Ben turned around to find his father with a big smile on his face. At this point, Ben felt that it was better for him to remain quiet and to find on his own the information he sought. So it was. Ben made it his goal to learn what was in that letter. Not only that, he also set a bigger goal of taking the letter to Gregorio and Kate, so as to help them. As he watched his father leave the room, Ben felt a certain confidence fill him. He was determined to have that letter between his fingers before he met the Tyler's the next morning. Ednesto had gently closed the door behind him, making sure that his son knew that he was leaving. Confident that his goal was achievable, Ben began brainstorming for a plan to get that letter and then take it to Kate.

"Father," Ben called out, running towards the closed door through which Ednesto had just passed. He opened the door, saw that his father was still in the hallway and walked up to him. "Hey, uh, I'd just like to apologize for the way I acted earlier. I was really—"

"I forgive you," Ednesto replied after he turned around to find his son in his nightclothes.

"Well," Ben said hesitantly, "if you forgive me, then why aren't you able to finish your story, please? I'm dying of curiosity. I can't just—" Once again, his father interrupted him, this time with an annoyed tone in his voice.

"Listen, just because I 'forgive' you doesn't mean that I will entrust you with *my* secret, okay?"

Nodding his head, Ben slowly whispered, "I understand." Ednesto was still suspicious about his son's strange behavior. Everyone who knew Ben knew that he was extremely stubborn and very hard to convince—but now, all of a sudden, he was giving in? That was a first for Ednesto. He said a quick good night and took off down the long, narrow hall.

"Wait!" Ben called after him, standing in the dark. "Can I at least have a hug—you know, a fatherly hug?" Any remaining doubt Ednesto still had about his son now vanished. Slowly, Ednesto began making his way back down the narrow hallway and to his waiting son. Ednesto admired the paintings hanging on the walls. He knew that something was up with his son, although for now he decided to keep it quiet and just let Ben do what he had to do. He hoped that this was just a phase. Once Ednesto was beside his son, Ben stretched his arms towards his confused father. After giving him a brief hug, which seemed to take forever, Ednesto removed his arms from his son, lightly nodded and quickly walked away towards his bedroom—before his son was able to call to him once again. As Ben headed back to his room, he felt a huge smile spreading across his face. It felt not only like a smile of accomplishment, but also like one of confidence. He was now convinced that he was able to set a goal and achieve it. Once back in his room,

Ben felt the cozy air on his body and prepared to throw himself down onto the comfortable sofa. First, though, he looked for a candle to provide light. Finding one candle, he placed it in a holder on the table near the sofa. He lit the wick. Around the candle was a decorative string. Ben had lit that, too, by accident. A fire started. Fortunately for Ben, there was a fireplace in his room. Without thinking twice, he threw the burning candle into the fireplace. "Finally," Ben whispered to himself as he clutched the letter between his fingers. "I finally did it. I accomplished something." Ben began untying the ribbon that had been wrapped a few times around the paper. His thoughts wandered back to his father's evil doings hours ago, when he had been with Isabella down in the dungeon. Just holding that ribbon made Ben shed a tear. *So much for letting your hair loose,* Ben thought as he placed the ribbon on the little end table next to the sofa. Afterward, he gently opened the letter and began to read, when he heard a gentle knock on the door. Ben was so frightened that his actions were quick. In less than three seconds, he had tied the ribbon in place, just as it was before, and put the letter in a cranny where even a tiny insect couldn't reach it. Casually, Ben approached the door and opened it slightly to find an empty hallway. Sure that he heard something; Ben stepped outside his room and looked around. Feeling a cold breeze, he began to turn back inside, anxious to continue reading the letter. Once he turned in the direction of his room, he realized that he was facing a closed door. Startled about what might have happened, he tried to enter his room, but someone was in there, behind the locked door. As Ben let out a sigh of obedience, he heard it flow through the hallway. The sigh's echo rang for about 10 seconds before fading.

"Oh, I just hope they don't find the letter," Ben said in a murmur. Minutes later, he was fast asleep in a guestroom.

As Rango searched Ben's room, his master went to see if Ben was sleeping. As Ednesto slowly opened the door to the guestroom, he heard a bang, as though something heavy had fallen to the ground. Frightened, he swung the door wide, looking for what had caused that sound. Glancing down, he saw his son lying there. Ben had fallen asleep against the door.

Rango entered the guestroom just then. "Leave him," Ednesto said as Rango tried to lift Ben.

"But, master, he's on the floor and—"

"I said to leave him," Ednesto interrupted him sharply. "If we move him, we risk waking him, and I certainly cannot take that chance. He has the letter, and I must find it before he awakes."

Rango just nodded.

"Well, then, let's continue our search," Ednesto said as he motioned his servant out of the guestroom and back to Ben's bedroom.

A while later, Rango threw himself on the sofa, making it clear that he had given up his search. "Clearly, the letter is not in this room. We've checked every corner; we've checked the closets, the chairs, the table and the sofa; and we even went through his thousand books. It's not here. What else would you have me do?" As Rango spoke, Ednesto began doubting that his son took the letter. Rango resumed speaking, as if he had read Ednesto's mind. "Are you sure he took the letter. Maybe you misplaced it. Maybe you—"

"No," Ednesto said rather loudly, trying to reassure himself. "When Ben 'awkwardly' asked me for a hug, I complied. That was probably when he took the letter from my cape pocket."

"Well, then, I guess we better keep—" Rango stopped in the middle of his sentence, as though he had just been startled by something.

"What's the matter?" Ednesto asked as he tried to see what held his servant's attention. Soon enough, they were both gazing at the same thing. "There is some wax among what looks to be fresh ash," Rango said at the fireplace. "What else but the letter would Ben have burned in the middle of the night?" Ednesto asked as he picked up a small handful of ash. "It looks like we have reached the end of our search here in this room. The letter is burnt." Ednesto nodded his head, although he seemed confused. "Why would he do such a thing?" Ednesto asked as he gathered his things to leave.

Rango replied, "Who knows?" As the two men exited the room, they each felt different emotions overcome them. Rango was relieved, and Ednesto was angry—although, at the same time, he was happy knowing that now the Tyler's would never be able to get their hands on that letter.

After they had gone, a large grin spread across Ben's face. Having hidden himself in the hallway, Ben now re-entered his room and felt that he had finally accomplished something.

Chapter 14

❧ • ❧

"And that is how I got the letter," Ben said as he looked at the note folded neatly in his hand.

"Wow, I really appreciate it," Kate said as she reached for the letter. "Oh, it was really no problem. That's what family does for each other," Ben replied.

"Family? We're not family. You're Ednesto's servant," Kate said, making it clear that she was confused. Knowing that he had just given away his secret, Ben quickly tried to find a way to cover his last few words. Yet, all he was able to do was laugh.

"When I said 'family,' I meant that Ednesto is your great-uncle, whose 'schemes' are devised to help you," Ben said, letting out another of his fake laughs. Kate knew that something was wrong with his explanation, although, luckily for Ben, she yearned to find out what was written in that letter more than anything at that present moment.

"So, will you let me read the letter?" Kate said while outstretching her hand.

"Oh yes, of course." Ben handed it over. As Kate held the paper close to her face, she was able to smell her mother's scent. For the first time since her journey had begun, she was able to *feel* her mother. Quickly enough, she untied the ribbon and opened the neat piece of paper. Once it was completely unfolded, her eyes moved from side to side, reading every word in the dark and foggy wet weather. It seemed that for every word she read, she shed another tear. When she finally finished with the letter, she practically knew it by heart. She then untied the other ribbon, the one inside the letter that contained the ring. Kate gently placed the ring on her thin finger. "It's a perfect fit," Ben said jokingly.

"It's beautiful," Kate said, as though she hadn't heard Ben's comment.

Feeling bad, Ben once again tried to cover his tracks. "It really is beautiful," he said. Kate smiled. Gregorio approached Kate and Ben, wearing his usual look of surprise. Before he was able to ask where he was, what he was doing there or any other of his usual questions, Kate began explaining everything. Yet again, Gregorio would ask if everything was fine; Kate would, of course, smile and say yes. By now, this was Kate's routine for conversing with her father. As Kate looked down at her ring, beautifully placed on her middle finger, she felt that there was nothing in the world she could do to repay Ben, so all she said was a kind thank-you.

"Oh, please, don't thank me. I'm sure you would do the same for me, right? Now, if you hadn't realized it, you don't have so much time at all, so I suggest that you get moving, find the next paper, solve the riddle and get to the next island." Still grateful to Ben, all Kate did was nod slightly. Then, taking his advice, she continued her journey across the island. The rain became stronger with every step they took. How Kate wished that her father hadn't wished for 'a little rain'! Her thoughts, however, didn't revolve around that. They revolved around the letter her mother had written for her. She felt happy that she was finally able to connect with her mom. Kate hadn't seen her mom for many hours. She keenly felt the responsibility of fighting for her mother's life. Plus, she only had a couple of hours left to reach the end of their journey.

"I can do it; I will do it," Kate whispered to herself as she walked through the ugly weather. Turning to see how her father was doing, she found him on the ground, sitting near a tree and trying to protect himself from the rain. Beside him was Ben, crouching. From what Kate could tell, Ben was trying to get Gregorio to stand. It didn't seem to be working, though. The stubborn Gregorio just lowered his head in confusion. When Ben saw that Kate was aware of the situation, he called her over.

"Listen, you have got to help me. I really want you to get your mother back. I really want you to succeed, but . . ."

Ben abruptly stopped speaking and turned his attention towards Gregorio. Gregorio said, "I'm sorry to have to put you through this. I feel so bad, especially since you do so much for me. You know what? I'm big enough to take care of myself. Just leave."

"What?" Ben asked curiously while looking at Kate, wondering if she would agree to her father's request.

Kate said to Ben, "No. Don't take what my father said in a bad way. Please understand. I see that you're concerned about us." Then she took Ben's place next to her father.

"Listen," Ben said, a wide smile on his face, "whether you want me to leave or not, I can't. Ednesto has forced me to stay. Remember, I'm his servant."

Kate nodded her head in understanding and grinned. That was what she had wanted to hear—that Ben would help her in the absence of her father's competent guidance. "Well, then, I guess we'll continue," Kate said while rising to her feet. As she and Ben began walking across the island searching for the next clue, Kate once again began to thank Ben. Just then, she heard a faint sound behind her. As she and Ben both turned to look, they realized that they had forgotten something: Gregorio. They quickly ran back towards him to find him lying straight out on the ground.

"What's the matter?" Ben and Kate said at the same time.

"I thought you forgot about me," Gregorio said. "Didn't you say that we're, like, family or something?" Feeling guilty, Kate helped her father up and once again began explaining to him that they were looking for a small piece of paper that would 'save their lives.'

"I don't want to get up. My clothes are soaked, which will make me catch a cold. I don't want that. Please understand."

Heartbroken, Kate quickly lifted the satchel her father had prepared and had drug all this way. Once Kate opened her father's bag, she began looking for a blanket or some clothing. Something in the satchel caught her eye: the golden horn that she had seen hours earlier. The horn was a big mystery to Kate. *What is the purpose of this horn?* Kate thought to herself as she pulled a clean pair of pants and a jacket from the bag. Why did her father want to keep it a secret? She definitely felt that the horn was magic, although she didn't know for what purpose. When Gregorio set eyes on the new set of clothing, his face lit up and he beamed with joy.

Chapter 15

❧ • ❧

Walking through the mud was difficult and took a long time. Their shoes and clothes were virtually destroyed. As the trio continued their journey to the other side of the island, they felt the impact of every raindrop. This, however, was nothing in comparison to what they would face next: silence.

Silence was the answer to the question. Silence was what they needed to find in order to get to the next island. Looking ahead in the downpour, they searched for where they were to head next. All three of them stopped abruptly. It dawned on them that they had found the island. As they waited for the canoe, they stared at the island in awe. Only then did they understand why it was called Silence. The entire island seemed to have been put on pause. The rain drops stood in the middle of the island, the sun had stopped shining overhead, and the clouds, which normally flew across the islands, just stood there. This, however wasn't the biggest surprise . . .

When the canoe arrived, Kate, the smallest, took her place in the front. Gregorio sat behind her. The tallest of the three, Ben, sat in the back. "So, what island?" the canoe driver asked as he began to paddle. None of them had heard him, though, because they were still in shock and staring. "Excuse me, sir, what island?" the driver asked again, this time expecting an answer from Ben.

"Oh, uh, sorry about that," Ben replied. "That one . . . isn't it obvious for it is the only one in sight" he said, pointing his index finger.

"Right away, sir," the canoe pilot replied.

Kate couldn't believe her eyes. Feeling that she had to say something, all that came out of her mouth was a simple "Wow."

"I know, it's unbelievable," Ben said, responding to Kate's comment. "How could something like this even exist?" she asked.

"Well," Ben said, sounding intellectual, "apart from being magic, this lake has very special power. Being the biggest lake in England has its advantages."

"Like?" Kate asked curiously, making it obvious that she wanted to know all about it.

"This lake is the largest in the country, which gives it the opportunity to have its own life. It's like—" Ben stopped for a moment, moving his eyes from side to side as he searched for the right words. "It's like this lake is its own person." Ben then ended his explanation and straightened himself in his seat. Moments later, he tilted his body to the side, as if having forgotten to tell Kate something. Seeing this, Kate turned around. "Plus, why do you think that this guy," he said, pointing to the driver, "isn't freaked out? He's used to this kind of thing. In fact, everyone who works here is used to it. Look."

For the first time, Kate realized that they were not alone on the island. Looking around, she saw people wearing grey T-shirts printed on the back with 'Windermere Lake Society.' "Wait. I thought that Ednesto had rented the whole island for task two," Kate said, looking around.

"Well," Ben began, "he did more than that. He actually bought the place." Shocked, Kate let her jaw drop.

Noticing her response, Gregorio asked, "Hey, are you all right, little girl?" Kate knew that whenever her father called her 'little girl,' it meant that he had no idea who she was, that he had once again forgotten everything. So, before he was able to ask his questions, Kate began answering them. This time, she answered him more quickly than she otherwise would have, as she was yearning to find out more about the island. When she was done with her explanations, she scooted her body so that she was now facing Ben.

"So, you mean to tell me that he owns this whole lake? How could that even be possible?" Kate asked, still shocked.

"Well, technically, he didn't permanently buy it. He bought it for task two, the terms stipulate that he will be the owner for as long as you are here." Nodding her head, Kate showed that she understood. "Only Ednesto," she said as she looked at the canoe pilot. *I wonder why he's still working here and why magic hasn't ruined his life,* Kate thought to herself, looking one more time at the man who was paddling the canoe. Then, without thinking twice, she asked the driver the question to which she ardently wished to know.

"Excuse me. Sir? I'm sorry if this question is too personal, but I'm really curious to know.

Are you a wizard?" Ben leaned to the right and looked at Kate with a facial expression that read, *Are you crazy?!*

Kate avoided making further eye contact with Ben and faced forwards for the rest of the ride. The man hadn't responded to her question, so she asked again, this time phrasing it differently. "Sir, I'm sorry to ask this question. It might be a little personal. But I was wonder—"

"I heard you ask the first time," the man said, smiling lightly as he fought against the strong wind.

"Oh, I'm sorry. I don't know what I was thinking. I shouldn't have asked."

"Don't worry," the driver said in a low voice. "You're not the first one."

"So, are you a wizard? I mean, I cannot imagine why a mortal would want to work in a place that is full of 'magic,'" Kate said, still facing the front of the canoe to avoid making eye contact with Ben.

"Well, the reason I work here is because of what happened to me many years ago." As he continued paddling the canoe, he began to tell an emotional, unforgettable story. "As a child growing up, I had a very hard life. I was born with one eye unable to see. Besides for being picked on as a young boy, I had it very hard when it came to dating. Even though I was still somewhat able to see, my vision was definitely not clear, for the eye that was working was not working 100%." He paused for a moment as he geared to the left. Then without further ado he continued. "I grew up in Belgium with my family who loved and cherished me very much. I was an only child so any thing I requested I received. My parents watched me live in misery; they threw their efforts into trying to satisfy me. Even though their actions meant a lot to me, my sentiments did not cease to worsen. One day we took a vacation here to England. My family being very touristic decided to visit Windermere Lake for it is the biggest lake! The moment we neared the lake and almost came in contact with it, a sensation I never felt before overpowered my body. I was all smiles! Seeing this, my parents drove faster until we finally reached the lake. The three of us quickly made our way out of the car to view the beautiful scenery. Being 18.08 km in length and 1.49 km in width, its dark blue waters swayed gently from side as the sunrays shone above them. With numerous islands residing on this beautiful island, their greenery was evident amongst the aqua waters brushing them. A few boats sailed through the island peacefully cutting through the current giving its onlookers a thirst to touch the silky waters. As the sun began to get warmer diamonds seemed to appear on the lake, swimming with ease in all directions they looked beautiful. I just stood and stared with fascination at this extravagant creation. Something about this island gave me the capacity to see every single detail encompassing it. The moment I discovered this I felt so exited and made the decision never to leave this island. Having so much pleasure here I wanted it to be permanent! My parents agreed right away wanting me to only be happy." He paused one more time, this time to retrieve his breath. Kate stared at him wide eyed begging for him to continue his intriguing story. "I soon found a small cottage to rent right by the lake, and just like I fantasized I spent my days here. I soon became a part of the lake by becoming a loyal employee of the Lake district. A couple of months ago I was threatened by a man to leave the island. Only in my nightmares did this occur although I prayed that this would never happen in real life. After much fighting and tears, the man agreed to have me work for him for free if I wished to remain on this island.

Agreeing to his request, little did I know it was three months of backbreaking work. Every time I asked for a break or a minimal amount of salary he threatened to burn my little house on the lake. I couldn't bear that horrendous idea and remained silent for the time being." As he finished his sentence they arrived to their next island. Before Kate was able to ask any questions he had already vanished

Chapter 16

❧ • ❧

"Wow! What an emotional story," Ben said as he walked towards the astonishing island. Ignoring the magnificent sights of the island, Kate's mind was still reflecting on his story.

"I guess so," Ben replied as he realized that he was standing in the most awesome place in the world. The entire island was silent. So silent it seemed evident to them from a distance!

"This place is amazing," Kate said, looking at Ben for a response. He didn't answer, so she repeated herself. Still, he barely even twitched. The next time she repeated her words, she nearly yelled. Ben remained quiet. After a few minutes, Kate realized that she was standing on an island of silence and that no one could hear her. *Great,* Kate thought to herself as she advanced towards Ben to 'tell' him again.

As she approached, he said, "Wait. What did you say?"

Confused, Kate was positive that she had said nothing. Then, Kate once again tried to speak. She opened her mouth, as she began to speak, her voice began to diminish, as though it was fading.

"Why did you say the *great*?" Ben asked, curious.

"I didn't *say* great. I *thought*—oh my gosh, you can hear my thoughts." Kate became aware that, on this island, her thoughts were not private. They were broadcast. "Why would Ednesto do such a thing? What does silence have to do with weather?" Kate asked in a tone that demanded an answer.

"Well," Ben began, unconfidently, "as you know, Ednesto is tricky and plays around with everything. Like, for example, take the word *weather*. It is defined as 'the state of the atmosphere with regard to temperature, cloudiness, rainfall, wind and other meteorological conditions.'"[1]

Kate wore an expression of confusion. "Okay, that's interesting. But what does it have to do with silence?"

---

[1] *Microsoft Encarta College Dictionary.* Soukhanov, Anne H., ed. New York: Macmillan, 2001.

Continuing to walk along the 'dead' island, Ben turned to look at Kate. "This is where silence comes in. The definition of *meteorological* is 'the scientific study of the earth's atmosphere.'[2] The definition of *atmosphere* is 'a prevailing emotional tone or attitude, especially one associated with a *specific* place or time.'"[3]

As Kate nodded her head in admiration, she thought to herself, *Wow, Ednesto is tricky. He pays attention to every single word.*

Oh yeah! Ben thought as he jumped up into the air to catch a frozen raindrop.

Kate nodded as she walked. She thought to herself that just by being on this island for a little while, she could write a book about how it looked. Everything was suspended. Even the air seemed frozen in time. Everything was pretty much dead. As Kate continued walking, she began thinking of her friend Lena, a girl in her class who was deaf and mute. In class, a woman would sit next to Lena and translate everything for her in sign language. Lena was an amazing girl with a sweet personality, although few people had discovered this fact, since hardly

---

[2] Ibid.
[3] Ibid.

anyone wanted to be friends with someone who couldn't speak or hear. Luckily, Kate had the chance to meet and get to know Lena. It took a while for Lena to open up, but once she did, the two girls became great friends. As their friendship began to grow, Lena had described to Kate (through lip reading) how it felt to be deaf and mute—and, as a result, how it felt to be ignored.

As much as Kate supported and loved her friend, she never was able to understand just how it was to be Lena. As many times as she tried to put herself in the other person's shoes, she still found herself saying, "I wish I could, but we have different shoe sizes. Your shoes won't fit me." Now, finally, on this island of silence, Kate was able to feel what it was like to be Lena. At last, she could fit into her friend's shoes. As she continued searching the island, she reflected more on the feelings of people who are deaf and mute. Not only that, but she also realized that this sojourn, this hard time she was enduring, had actually taught her many life lessons. Her attitude became more positive. She began to realize that no matter how bad her life may be, there was always something or someone worse. Kate vowed always to find the good, no matter what. She interrupted her own line of thinking with, *how in the world are we supposed to find the note?*

"This place is so silent that the clue is probably between two blades of grass somewhere," Gregorio thought, making it clear by his facial expressions that he was talking to Ben.

"I get you, buddy. No one can understand Ednesto. He's just so—well, what can I tell you? That's life, and—"

"No," Kate interrupted as Ben was thinking. *"You can't say that! You can't say, 'That's life.' Do you know that out there in the world are thousands of people dying of sickness and thousands of orphans we should at least be thankful to have—"* Right then and there, Kate realized that she had said something unacceptable. She had forgotten that Ben had no parents. She began apologizing. *I'm so sorry; I completely forgot,* her facial expression read.

"What are you talking about?" Ben replied. *"I mean, it's okay. Don't worry about it."* As Kate continued apologizing, *"Please stop apologizing,"* he said in his mind.

Phew, I'm glad to have gotten her to stop apologizing, and I'm happy that she is off my back, Ben thought to himself, forgetting that his thoughts were broadcast. Kate had heard him.

Excuse me? You're telling me that you don't mean what you just said? That you said it for no apparent purpose? Kate thought, making it clear that she was offended.

"Listen, I didn't mean to. I just—"

I heard what you thought. You can't hide it, Kate thought for Ben's benefit, beginning to walk away from him and towards the isthmus. She then stopped and waited for his explanation. The silence caused the air to thicken. Clearly, Ben had nothing to say, so Kate turned her back to him and ran in the opposite direction.

"Be careful, Kate. Don't go to that island. It's dangerous out there." By the time Ben finished his sentence, Kate was already out of his sight. She had not heard his warning. As she walked towards the dangerous island, she became more and more frightened.

Chapter 17

Placing his right hand on the kitchen counter, he dialed a familiar number with his left. The phone rang a few times before a sweet voice answered.

"Hey, Veronica, how are you doing in your travels?" Ednesto said to his wife, practically leaning on the counter.

"Hi, honey, how are you? We will soon be heading to Australia. I'm so excited. I heard it's a beautiful place filled with happiness on every corner," Veronica answered enthusiastically as she closed her suitcase for the next journey.

"It sure is a beautiful place. I'm so confused about where you are lately. It's so hard to keep track of your destinations. It's also hard having a wife who is a flight attendant."

"Well, what can I say? It's a job I have loved doing ever since I was 18."

Ednesto flashed back to when he and his wife first met. "Hey, Ver, are you thinking what I'm thinking?" he said as he grabbed a chair to sit by the phone.

"It seems just like yesterday, doesn't it?" his wife said, also thinking of how they first met.

It was 1995. Ednesto had finally earned his flying license. He had, at last, become a pilot. As a young 19-year-old, he began working for Yale Airlines. He was known as an amazing pilot, flying all over the world and never encountering any difficulties or problems that he couldn't handle. He was known as one of the best until the day when he was assigned to a flight to Africa. Very excited, since it was his first time flying to Africa, he boarded the plane with his co pilot. Just minutes before they were scheduled to take off, Ednesto once again checked that he was ready. About 15 minutes later, the plane began moving down the runway. It followed the orange lines and then lifted off, flying in the direction of the designated destination. Once in the air, the plane flew smoothly above the thick, white clouds. Everything was under control. The pilot turned off the seat belt lights. The passengers felt at ease. After nine hours in the air, the plane began to shake, slightly at first. Then, the shaking became obvious. Passengers began to panic. Ednesto quickly began checking the control buttons. A little red flashing light at the corner of the control board caught his eye.

As he looked closer, he realized that the plane was dropping fuel. At this point, Ednesto knew that it was going to crash. All 500 passengers aboard that plane would be gone in a short time. Not only would Ednesto be responsible for the passengers' deaths, but he would also bring his own life to an end.

Ednesto then began to make an announcement. As the passengers eagerly awaited news, they were silent. Once the captain's shaky voice began speaking, the travelers were all ears.

"Attention, passengers. We have good news and bad news. The good news is that we're landing immediately. The bad news is that we're crash landing." People screamed and babies cried. Some passengers prayed. Even the atheist on board began crying out to G-d for help. No one in the cabin was spared from experiencing a breakdown. Couples began spilling their secrets to one another. Children said their good-byes. Then, the aircraft turned upside down, 35,000 feet above Earth. Soon enough, the plane had lost considerable altitude. Its nose sped towards the ground below: Abidjan in Côte d'Ivoire. The speed was so intense that a few of the passengers lost their ability to hear. While

Ednesto had tried his best to pull the plane out of the nosedive, he realized now that there was nothing more he could do. The plane crashed and split in half.

People were silent. The majority of passengers had survived. They just sat in their seats, in shock. Staff members issued instructions. The aircraft's fuselage was almost detached. As Ednesto sat in his seat, the plane's electricity cut out. With no lights, it was pitch-black. No one moved. Luckily for the crew and passengers, the plane had crashed when it was daylight.

Ednesto began to cry. Slowly leaning against the window, he saw that the plane's flaps were smoking. In a few minutes, he reasoned, the aircraft would catch on fire and explode. Frightened, Ednesto realized that this was his chance to save the passengers. He rapidly opened the door outside the cockpit and ran out. A huge yellow slide inflated at the door and unfurled towards the ground. He was now somewhat able to see the damage to the airplane. In a deep voice, he called for the crew members. Following his voice, they found him beside the door. Parents clutched their children and couples held each other close, hoping to make it out alive. Urging people to hurry, the flight attendants followed the pilot's instructions for the passengers' safe exit. Many tended to their children or the elderly, leaving only a few people focused on those who were injured.

Only one crew member remained to take care of the traumatized pilot: Veronica, a young flight attendant, has known Ednesto by name for quite a while. From the very beginning of this haunting episode, she stayed by his side, motivating him with words of encouragement and ensuring him that he would hold on and make it through this catastrophe with his sanity intact. At the time, Ednesto seemed oblivious of Veronica. Later, he was thankful to her. If it hadn't been for her, he would have never been able to get through the experience and maintain his lucidity.

It took nearly 20 minutes to get the passengers out of the plane. Another seven minutes passed as the injured made their way out. While the operation was concluded in less than half an hour, to live it seemed like forever. The conscious voyagers were tempted to hug the ground the moment they stepped foot on it. The crowd erupted in gratitude for; they had made it out alive. As they cheered and sang out, the pilot, all smiles, made his way out of the plane. He was accompanied by Veronica, his friend, his stewardess and, most importantly, his fiancée.

Chapter 18

Ednesto held the receiver tightly in his hand, positive that Veronica was smiling. The story of how they met and fell in love would always be precious to them. They kept it forever in their hearts. Hoping to finish the conversation with his wife, Ednesto excused himself, saying that he had to hang up. After he and Veronica exchanged good-byes, they got off the phone.

The story of how they met ended there for Veronica, but for Ednesto, it was far from over. Finally safe on an emergency helicopter, they flew towards there initial destination: Johannesburg, South Africa. At last arriving at the airport, the fleet of emergency helicopters filled with passengers landed safely, thank G-d. The one carrying Ednesto and Veronica landed safely, too. As they began their descent, Ednesto noticed that near the airport, awaiting them, stood the owner, the president and the manager of Yale Airlines. *Yes!* Ednesto thought. *I'm finally going to receive my first badge from the owner, president and manager. This must be huge.* It was huge, but not in the way Ednesto expected it to be. Finally off the helicopter, Ednesto put on his hat and, like a gentleman, walked towards the three men.

"Hello, sir. I suppose you're here to see me?" Ednesto asked the owner as he straightened out his uniform.

"We sure are," the owner answered coldly, firmly shaking Ednesto's hand.

"I'm sorry, sir. I can't hear you. The noise is too loud for me to—" He was interrupted by the three men nodding their heads and motioning with their hands for him to enter the airport. Once inside the perfectly temperate lounge, the four of them sat down on large leather sofas arranged around a small table filled with finger foods. As Ednesto enjoyed the olives and nuts, he sat there with a big smile, thinking that this might be the beginning of a new career for him.

"So, what is all this about?" Ednesto couldn't help but ask. Again, the response from the three men was absolute silence. At this point, Ednesto realized that they hadn't called this meeting for the reasons he had supposed. As he slowly placed his plate on the table, he noticed one of the men stand and gaze at him. Ednesto lifted his head at the president's approach. Frightened to speak, Ednesto then lowered his head and remained in that posture for a few moments, until he felt the president's hand touch his chest and unpin the wings from Ednesto's uniform.

"My wings," Ednesto managed to say, almost whispering the words.

"We're really sorry. You don't deserve them. It has been proven to us that a young man like you is way too young to fly, that—"

"Then why did you give them to me?" Ednesto interrupted him angrily. "Why would you do such a thing to me?"

"I guess," the owner began. He soon stopped, as though the words had faded on his lips because it was too painful for him to speak his mind.

"You guess what?" Ednesto said, his eyes tearing up.

"Well," the manager began as he popped an olive into his mouth, "when we first received your application to be a pilot for Yale Airlines, we were hesitant to hire a 2 year experienced man and entrust him with hundreds of lives. We weren't sure until we thought of—"

"Until you thought of my brother," Ednesto said suddenly.

"That is correct," the owner said, smiling thinly.

"Although we are now certain that you are clearly not like your brother," the president said coldly, placing his right arm on his right knee.

"We're sorry. We thought we could trust you, but we have determined now that we clearly cannot," the owner said, waving the pilot wings at Ednesto.

"It isn't fair to compare me to my brother. I'm my own person. You have to accept that. Now, if you would please give me back my wings, I'll forget this ever happened," Ednesto said in a hopeful tone.

"You see, that's the problem. You might forget that this incident happened, although we won't—"

"It was just a little crash," Ednesto said, arrogance in his voice, yet knowing deep down inside that it was indeed not a "little" crash it was extreme.

"A little crash?" the president yelled at him. "A little crash that will cost our company millions. Not only have we lost a plane, but we also have to insure everyone who was victimized. You think that is easy?"

"Oh, please, your company is a multimillion-dollar one. You aren't able to pay for a simple plane crash? You're always saying that you make so much money and that you're the best. Plus, I saved those people on the plane! It's not like they're all dead!"

"True. You might have saved those people. But the few who remained may be scarred for life. Those people will never forget it. *Plus,*" the president said, mimicking Ednesto's tone of arrogance, "the people who lived through this crash will remain too traumatized to fly with us again, which will result in our losing hundreds of customers—since their families and friends will be traumatized, as well." The president spoke these words so confidently that Ednesto began to feel guilty. But his sense of guilt didn't stop him from arguing his point.

"It's really not that bad, I'm sure that—"

"*That's enough,*" the owner yelled, frightening everyone. "Listen, we're really sorry, but you will never be as good as your brother. It was our mistake in hiring you. I guess, well, I guess that we thought you were different . . ." At this point, a tear of anger dripped down Ednesto's face. As he walked away, he vowed never to let those words escape his mind: *You will never be as good as your brother.* That was the day when he decided to get back at his brother, for something his brother never did, to get something that he didn't have, for something his brother never did: the family powers. As these thoughts raced through Ednesto's mind, the three men just sat there. Each had a different background and a different life, but they all had one thing in common: they were all the oldest among their siblings and had never known the feeling of being young and wanting to achieve something but not being able to.

This day was when it all began, when many lives will change: Ednesto's life, his brother's life, Isabella's life, Gregorio's life and, most importantly, Kate's life.

*   *   *

Once she reached the other side of the island, Kate walked around with numerous emotions bundling up inside of her. She wasn't able to tell whether it was fear or pain. She remained confused as she continued searching for the letter. After a while, she reflected to her fight with Ben. Reviewing the situation, she was still unable to figure out what he had been thinking. She sat down on a rock. *He said something about an actress. Or did he say that I was brainless? Maybe he wants me to become a seamstress. What was it?*

Kate remembered hearing the urgency in his voice. She was sure that what Ben had thought rhymed with one of the words that had just crossed her mind. What could it possibly be? What could possibly lead Ben to saying something with such urgency? *I guess I'll find out soon enough, if it is really that important,* Kate thought to herself. Just then, she saw something that made her think of the word: *dangerous.*

The rock upon which she was sitting began to sink. Kate knew that she was not in the best place. Quickly, she jumped off the rock. When she hit the ground, she was relieved to be safe. The rock began sinking into quicksand. "Phew, I'm saved," she was surprised to find herself saying. "Wow, I guess this island isn't all mute," she jokingly said to herself as she continued walking, this time more cautiously and alert to any potential surprises.

Kate felt that her being on that little piece of land would do nothing for her. All she was doing was burning time. She shortly realized, that she was trapped on a dangerous island that would bring nothing but horror. As she walked through the island in fear she heard a loud growl which confirmed her panic. At first, she decided that her imagination had conjured up the growl, and so she ignored it. Once she had heard the growl several more times, she was positive that there was an animal somewhere amongst the trees. Even while knowing that something was just beyond the trees, she sincerely believed that she wouldn't be harmed—until she saw a pair of green eyes staring at her through the bushes.

"Oh no, what do I do!?" she said to herself, panicking. Kate froze in place and felt an eerie sensation in her bones. A shiver of absolute terror rolled down her back. At this point, she was only concerned with the animal hiding behind those bushes. Because Kate loved to research, she knew practically everything there was to know about pretty much everything, animals included. She trained her eyes on the small openings between the high bushes but couldn't see anything until the animal began to move. Kate was now standing face-to-face with a puma. "That's weird. I didn't know pumas lived on islands . . . in *England!*" She soon realized that was definitely the worst first impression she could've had. Without thinking twice, she ran for her life, despite the fact that it was an unwise thing to do. Kate knew very well that whenever one was in the presence of an animal and was frightened, one should never show fear, since predatory animals are always, in all circumstances, able to sense it. Once they sense a person's fear, they attack. It was out of fear that Kate had begun to run, even though she thought that pumas rarely attacked human beings. Kate rationalized that what she was doing was fine. As she continued running, she heard the puma's footsteps behind her. Now, she was convinced that it was all over, that she was going to die. As Kate surrendered, she sat on the ground facing the thumping footsteps. To her surprise, she saw an empty forest. Empty except for the thumping sounds.

Chapter 19

The thumping continued. Kate's heart beat faster by the second. She feared the worst. Suddenly, she felt fur on the top of her head. Even though it lasted for a split second, her sensation of terror lasted for much longer. Kate was certain that something had jumped over her. She was certain that she had felt fur. And, of course, she was now doubly sure that she was on a dangerous island.

"Where in the world did you come from?" Kate said in an angry voice as she got up and ran towards a rock a few yards away. Making it safely to the rock, she watched as the rock on which she previously sat, got swallowed by the quicksand. "Wow, that was close," Kate whispered as she jumped off the rock once more, this time aiming for the green grass. As she continued walking along the island, it came to her knowledge that this was a part of the lake that Ednesto didn't own, for it was clearly not "muted" and, therefore he couldn't control it. For the first time since the 11-hour countdown had begun, she felt free. Kate had a passion for exploring. Always curious, she couldn't help but wonder what was behind this or that rock, what this or that person was thinking or even

why she was named Kate. Nothing stopped
the young girl from finding answers to the
questions that emerged in her mind. Now, Kate
explored every rock, every tree, every insect—
practically everything. She walked around the
island mesmerized until something caught her
eye close to where she was standing. As she
approached, she saw a pole erect in the middle of
the island.

That's strange! Kate thought to herself as
she began retracing her steps in her mind. She
was sure that she had not seen a pole on any
of the other islands she had been on today. It
was abnormal. *Although*, she figured, *if it's here,
it's here for a reason.* Approaching the pole, she
realized the reason for its being there. On the
tall pole was a sign that read, "Warning! This
island may be swallowed up by the tide! Beware,
you never know what may hit you . . . the island
is usually swallowed every 11 years. —Written
on May 7, 2003(even though it reappears)"

As Kate stood before the crinkled paper
sign, she felt indifferent. While anyone else
would be intrigued, Kate—considering all that
she had encountered so far—felt that this was
just another drop in her already overflowing
cup. She was not startled by the dire warning.

One of Kate's fears was of being buried alive. She had already been buried alive, in a manner of speaking, when she had found herself under water. She pushed that thought aside and continued her stroll. Even though she saw the water level rising, she wasn't bothered. She continued to enjoy the view: trees, shiny rocks, and the puma—the puma! Still frightened, she was aware of every step she took. Literally not taking her eyes off the island, Kate turned her head every so often. After a while, her neck began to ache. She finally gave up and came to the wise conclusion that staying on this island was the opposite of being on vacation, as all she experienced here was fear and unpleasantness. Once she made up her mind to leave the island, she retraced her footsteps and returned to the place from where she had started. As she encountered the quicksand again, she realized that there was no way off of this small piece of land. She was trapped.

"If I'm trapped, then how was it possible for me to get onto this island?" Kate asked herself. Apparently, the puma had heard her.

"Oh no," Kate said, moments after realizing that she had just made a mistake. She then began running for her life. She dashed so quickly along the side of the island and thought that maybe the puma hadn't seen her. The reality was quite the opposite: she hadn't seen the puma. After running a bit farther, all she began to see was green bushes, they soon made there way toward Kate to prick her, the fear overcoming her was overpowering. Tears filled her eyes. She began noticing all sorts of insects, all sorts of animals. Until—she grew tired and stopped. Fortunately for her, after using numerous wise technics to avoid the animal, the fascinating puma had also grown tired of running and had given up.

After unsuccessfully finding the entrance she had used to get on the island, she came to conclusion that it was gone. *How can that be possible?* she wondered. She remembered entering the island through a small passage that had somehow been connected to the other island she had been on with Ben and her father. As she once again searched the small piece of land, turning her head to examine the place where the small passage had been before, she concluded that the entryway had somehow disappeared. Then, she nearly jumped in fright as she beheld the implicit answer to her question: the water level had risen so high that it had practically swallowed the little passage that had been there a short time ago. She decided that she had to get off of the island before she herself was consumed. *What does a person do in a situation like this?* she thought. *Where can I go?* It was hopeless to hide. Just then, she remembered reading, "It's not the load that breaks you; it's the way you carry it." Thus, Kate decided to carry her load in the right way, with confidence and determination, until she was relieved of her burden. These thoughts, however, came was too late. The water now reached Kate's feet. She followed her gut instinct and ran with all her might all the way across the island, trying her best to avoid the water, which was about to pour in on her. What she feared most was not getting into the water on time, but she didn't let her fearful mind rule her determined heart. She continued running as the water swallowed the island.

Kate had jumped off the island and into the lake at the last second. Nervous about being swallowed, she had fallen on her stomach, which caused her pain. Her gut still throbbing, the preteen turned around to see a big splash. She laughed because the splatter resembled a mushroom. At this time, Kate felt many emotions, including relief. She convinced herself that everything would be fine. Happy but confused, Kate forced her body to swim against the tide, it was extremely frightening, especially now, it was night time and very dark! Lest it prevented her from reaching the island she was swimming towards. It was difficult to swim for so long in such choppy water. Kate's body felt painful. Inside, she felt frustrated and insecure. At this point, Kate finally gave up.

"There's only so much I can do," she said as she let the tide take her body wherever it wished. Casting off the feeling of frustration, Kate relaxed, now totally trusting in G-d. As her body moved with the tide, she felt that was in the Dead Sea. Memories flashed in her mind. Kate envisioned her mother as she closed her eyes to enjoy the memory of her dear mother. Not a single moment passed when Kate didn't think about her mother.

"You never know how precious your things are until you lose them," Kate whispered, a tear flowing down her unusually pale, delicate cheek. This had become Kate's motto. As she began to cough, she realized that maybe it hadn't been such a good idea to let the tide take her. She began to swallow water. Once again, Kate tried to fight the tide; once again, she failed. Too tired to continue, Kate still refused to give up, although at this point she felt that she had no choice. She flowed with the strong tide and, from time to time, swallowed more water. Moments later, she felt her skin touch something hard, something that was definitely not water. Too tired to stand, Kate moved her hand to feel what she was lying on. It was sand.

Aware that she was on an island, she quickly forced her body to rise. She hoped that she was on the right island, or, at least, near it. Elevating her head, Kate noticed two figures moving in the distance. Trying to adjust her eyes to determine their identity, Kate struggled, as a lot of water had entered her body. Finally able to focus, Kate saw that the two people were her father and Ben.

Thank you, thank you so much, Kate thought as she lifted her head in gratitude to G-d. Moments later, the two men noticed her. Noticing her pale face (even in the dark), confirmed that something was wrong. Already with many troubles on his mind, Ben took care of Kate with as much patience and delicacy as she needed. Soon enough, she was back on her feet and walking. "Thank you. I much appreciate it," Kate tried to say, although she realized that no voice escaped her mouth. She rethought her words to communicate to Ben.

"Don't thank me. I'm the one that should be thanking you," Ben *said* as he wiped his forehead, as if he had just done hard work.

"Thank me? What for?" Kate said needlessly, since her facial expression said it all.

"For what? Well, for coming back, of course. I was positive that you were not going to get back on time. It was hard taking care of a man with amnesia. I admire your patience in this situation. I honestly don't know how you do it," Ben thought to her as they walked along the island.

"Well, thank you. I admire you for staying strong while I was gone, and also for not giving up," Kate said, smirking. Feeling awkward, Kate quickly changed the subject to something much more important. *"So, uh, not to stress you or anything, but did you, by any chance—"*

"Find the letter? The next clue? Sure did," Ben said, interrupting her thoughts.

"Oh, thank you! I was so worried the whole time. Thank you so much."

"Will you stop thanking me, already?" Ben said as he once again interrupted her.

Still smiling, Kate continued. *"So, did you figure out the answer to the question?"* Kate asked with a hopeful smile.

"Well, there's a little problem," Ben said as he walked away from her, obviously trying to avoid answering.

"So?" Kate said, pushing him to answer. She faced him, her desire to know the answer palpable. *"Don't tell me you lost the letter?"* Kate said as her eyes moistened and her checks flushed.

"No, it's not that. Don't worry, the letter is perfectly fine," Ben reassured her. Then, he produced the letter from his pocket.

"What is it, then?" Kate said, completely confused.

"It's worse. The letter is . . ."

"The letter is . . . ? Come on. Go ahead. You'll eventually have to tell me, anyways," Kate pressed as she stood in front of Ben, blocking his way.

"The letter is blank."

Chapter 20

As she heard Ben's thoughts, Kate's facial expression resembled the letter. It was blank. She shook her head in denial. *"It can't be blank! No! It absolutely cannot be blank! Are you sure that it's the paper? Maybe you found another letter, another paper. I'm sure—"* This time, she was interrupted by the look on Ben's face. He wore a simultaneously guilty and innocent expression, which caused her to stop in mid-sentence. Still confused, she slowly resumed speaking. *"What's up?"*

With an amused grin on his face, Ben slowly held out the paper before her eyes, making it apparent that he was about to offer an explanation. *"You see this paper?"* Kate nodded. *"Well, this paper is the paper that Ednesto made for us. My proof is that on the back, he signed his name, just like he did on all of the other papers,"* Ben said, flashing a sideways grin as he brought the collection of papers from his pocket.

"That's just . . . great! When I thought that things would finally work out, this has to—" Kate interrupted herself. Something seemed to have caught her eye. Whatever it was, it was certainly

important; otherwise, the young girl would have never grabbed the paper from Ben's hand. *"Wait a second, this paper is blank . . . Blank."* Baffled, Ben watched his cousin run towards her father, who was carrying her backpack. Kate felt relieved that she had left her backpack with her father, as it contained many things she needed. As Kate searched her backpack, she felt the numerous objects inside it, eventually feeling the music box. At that moment, she felt the world freeze. Nothing else was important to her. It was just her and the music box. As she dug her head into her oversize backpack, she enjoyed hearing the beautiful melody playing on the beautiful gold music box. Still felt that it was a confirmation that her mother was still alive. Feeling eyes on her back, Kate turned to look and then saw Ben gazing at her in confusion. She felt herself blush. Noticing the moonlight from the sun shining above her, all she was able to do was nod her head. Ben felt her emotions: she was indifferent. Kate stood. Holding the music box tightly in her hand, she advanced towards Ben, smiling innocently.

"What's that you got there?" Ben asked, curious, wondering what Kate had been doing with her head stuck in her backpack. Deciding that it was not the right time to ask her, he

placed the thought aside, although he still
intended to solve the mystery.

"*Well,*" Kate said, clearing her throat and
placing the music box on a rock beside Ben,
"*when you showed me the letter, for you it might
have seemed empty. But I saw some letters. Take
a look for yourself.*" Ben looked more puzzled
than ever. He was sure he had seen a blank
piece of paper. How did Kate see something? He
had nothing to lose by looking, so he did. To his
surprise, he found that there was something
written on the paper that he held lightly
between his fingers. "*Seeing that gave me the
solution to this problem,*" Kate said. Then, with
an air of confidence, she set the music box away
from Ben. As he slowly took a different object
from Kate's hand, he examined it. It was a pen.
On the side, printed in a tiny font, were the
words 'Invisible ink.'

"*No way! Where did you get this? I thought
you guys didn't have powers! Or, at least, cool
objects with powers!*" Ben said as he tested the
pen on a rock.

Kate laughed as she began to explain.
"*The pen you see right here has nothing to do with
powers or magic. It's simply a scientific invention.*

Invisible ink dates as far back as the first century, when Roman officer Pliny the Elder explained how the milk of the thithymalus plant could be used for invisible ink. During the American Revolution, British and American spies used a mixture of ferrous sulfate and water to create invisible ink. In the 19th century, Henry Solomon Wellcome, a pharmaceutical entrepreneur, was just 16 when he advertised his invention, Wellcome's Invisible Ink. Invisible ink was also used in the Indian Mutiny of 1857 for covert messages; rice starch was applied and developed by means of iodine. During the late 19th and early 20th century, carbon copies were used for secret writing. The CIA used this method, using paper that contained a special chemical that would invisibly transfer to a second sheet of paper. The message could then be developed by using water or heat. This led to—"

"Wow! You seem to know a lot of about invisible ink. I see that history is really your thing," Ben interrupted. Kate had learned about the history of invisible ink because she had researched it after having bought the pen. Kate felt a need to be knowledgeable about the objects she owned. Other people might think it strange, but she believed that to own an object, one should know its history.

"*So, as I was saying, years after invisible ink was invented, someone had the bright idea to put it in pens.*"

Nodding his head in admiration, Ben said, "*I see. That sounds very interesting.*" Ben's tone was mocking, although Kate clearly was unable to realize it.

She continued. "*It sure is. Since I bought this pen, I have used it to write personal notes—*"

"*That's why your diary was empty!*" Ben said, sounding as if he had just found the missing piece to a puzzle.

"*Oh my goodness! You read my diary?*" "Uh, well . . . I mean—*"

"You mean nothing! Like I told you previously, there's nothing you can hide on this island. I can read your mind!"

"*Why do you care, anyway? I didn't even get to read 'invisible ink,' remember?*" Ben said as he waved the pen before her eyes.

"*If you read it or not is not the point. Your purpose was to eventually read it—and that's what makes me mad*!" Kate said angrily. Ben smiled slightly. "*Oh, I'm sorry, you think this is funny? This is anything but funny*!" Still laughing, Ben kept quiet. "*Let's just please get to business and finish this task*," Kate concluded.

Adopting an air of sophistication, Ben nodded his head and motioned for Gregorio to take a seat beside him. Gregorio, once again, began explaining his situation to Ben, which was a story Ben practically knew by heart.

Ben said, "*Okay, I am now ready to solve the riddle. How do we find the question? Are there particular glasses we should wear that will help us in finding the answer? Or is it—*"

"*No.*" Kate had interrupted Ben once again. Annoyed, he let her carry on with her explanations. "*The way our eyes will be able to see this imperceptible ink is by using this special light.*"

Kate paused and watched Ben as the information began to sink in. Soon enough, he motioned with his head for her to continue. "*Furthermore, this ink doesn't stay for long. After a while, it fades away, disappears—*"

"*Oh no!*" Ben quickly interrupted. "*Quick! Shine a light on it, quick.*" Obeying his orders, Kate quickly straightened out the paper on the rock. Frustrated because it was still crumpled, Kate nearly ripped it. Ben came to the rescue, placing his fingertips at the edges of the paper to make it easier for Kate to smooth it. Once Kate aimed the light at the paper, she saw faint letters appear. Then, she was barely able to see anything. Confused, Kate shone the light on the paper once more and tried to read, but she still saw no words.

Seeing the confused look on her face, Ben said, "*Let me see that.*" Taking the paper between his hands, he lifted it and then repositioned it to face in his direction. Leaning in to look, he tenderly motioned for Kate to hand over the light. She placed it in his hands. He lowered his head in complete concentration and pressed the little round button beneath the miniature light bulb. Amazed at this invention, he began switching the light on and off, until he felt eyes upon him. He lifted his head to find Kate gazing at him, annoyed. "*Sorry about that. I was just—*"

"*Just continue, and please try to figure it out. Right now, we're—*" Kate paused, looked at her father and quickly corrected herself. "*Sorry,*

191

I meant that I'm in desperate need of help. Just do anything! Anything to find the answer, which will hopefully—"

"*Wow, this is awesome!*" Ben said. Once again realizing that he was not doing what he was supposed to be doing, he refocused his attention. He shone the light on the paper, trying hard to make out any words. It seemed impossible. As he continued moving the pen along the corners, he began to see other letters, other words. Then he saw another sentence. Happy that he was able to help and reveal half the paper, he showed it to Kate.

"I am bigger than my friend," the paper read.

After Kate read that sentence, she was determined to find out it's meaning. With only two hours and a half remaining, she knew that she had to. There was no other choice.

Chapter 21

"'*T . . . e, o . . . a . . . n.' what was he thinking when he wrote this*?" Ben said as he tried to decipher the rest of the sentence.

"*By the look of things,*" Kate said, walking around the rock to get closer to Ben, "*this clue was written not too long ago, maybe a few hours, I'd say*!"

"*I guess you're right, although this right here,*" Ben said, his index finger pointing to the side of the paper with the 'clear' writing which said, 'I am bigger than my friend.'" *Hmm,* Ben thought to himself, rubbing his chin. "*I see that this part,*" he said, tapping the right side of the paper, "*was written not too long ago, which would explain why it is clearly visible*!"

"*Ha! I guess that Ednesto isn't that smart! He can never completely fool us,*" Kate said.

"*True. I guess we're just too good for him*!" Ben replied.

Kate began laughing a counterfeit laugh. Deep down, she was very frightened and knew that Ednesto would always find a way to fool them.

*   *   *

As the knocking grew louder, Ednesto became annoyed and soon dragged himself towards the shaking door. "I'm coming, I'm coming," the irritated man said, turning the doorknob to allow his tired son to enter. "I thought I gave you the key. Didn't I?" he said with a curious smile, motioning for Ben to come in.

"Uh, I don't think so. Then again," he added as he took a seat next to his father on the couch, "I might have lost it along the way. You know, walking across those islands is tiring and a tad irritating." Ben smiled crookedly and straightened his dirty shirt.

"So, Son, are you following our plan?"

"Plan?" Ben asked, looking confused. Realizing that he had made a mistake, Ben quickly said, "Yeah, sure."

"Good, good," his father said, nodding his head. Ednesto was not convinced. "So, how did you start the conversation? I mean, what did you tell them?"

"Uh, well, I started off with a simple greeting."

"Saying?" Ednesto asked inquisitively, urging his son to continue.

"Well, moments after I introduced myself, I told them my 'life story.' I—"

"You told them what?" his father asked in complete shock. He then coughed loudly and choked on the water he had just drunk.

"Don't worry, Father. I told them the other story, you know . . ." *The other story full of lies,* Ben thought.

Ednesto nodded his head to show Ben that he was proud of him.

It was normal for a father to be proud of a son who behaved in a kind way, brought home a good report card or a good behavior. Ben was disgusted to find that his father was proud of him for lying. He felt hurt and wished he was able to have a normal life. As he daydreamed, he felt his thoughts wonder off far, far away. He sensed that he was so distant from 'the real world' that no one could bring him out of his reverie. No voice could disturb him, except one.

"Ben!" Ednesto called out loudly. Feeling the blood rush to his cheeks, Ben quickly turned towards his father. Feeling embarrassed, he told his story. Once finished, he anxiously waited for his powerful father to reply. After a few long moments, Ednesto replied with a slight smile that morphed into laughter, which ended when Ben stared bluntly at his father in complete confusion.

"I am completely taken aback by what you told me!"

"I can see that," Ben said, mystified. "I wasn't aware that I was a comedian," he added with a slight yet confused smile. As Ben's mirrored him, the young man felt befuddled.

"Oh, you thought I was talking about . . . oh no!" Ednesto cut himself off and giggled. "I was talking about the story that you invented to tell the Tyler's. You told them that you 'created' the three tasks, correct?"

"Yes," Ben answered slowly, still unsure why his father was unusually jolly.

"Well, that is the exact reason I am laughing. I cannot believe that they actually believed that you were wise enough to invent those tasks."

At that moment, Ben felt embarrassed. As he listened to his father criticize him, one spiteful comment after another, he felt the lump in his throat enlarge. Every second that passed saw his face turn a different shade, beginning with light pink and ultimately changing to red once his father was done. Ben was sensitive, soft and, at times, unmanly. This was one of the times.

As his eyes turned red, Ben felt himself force the tears from making their way across his face. Each time he witnessed see the relationship between Kate and her father, he desired to have what she did. For Ben, it wasn't even an option to be close to his father. It wasn't even an option to talk to him. It was tough.

After his father had concluded his speech of condemnation, Ben felt the blood drain from his face. It became as pale as his father's white shirt. Ben knew that when a person felt embarrassment, it was like being killed in that all the blood rushes up to the face and then, moments later, drains, leaving the face pale. He spoke. "Well, I just felt I needed to tell them that so they would let me tag along and so I would be able to—"

"Excuse me. What do you mean, 'tag along'? The reason I sent you down there is so you could interfere with their tasks and make them lose time, not so you could tag along."

"I understand," Ben said awkwardly, trying to avoid eye contact with his father. If he did, his father would find out the truth. Aware that the eyes are the windows of the soul, Ben knew that if his father looked into his eyes, he would see what Ben was hiding.

"So," Ednesto said, "I assume that what you do is fundamentally try to confuse them with regard to the tasks." Noticing that his son didn't answer, he loudly added, "Am I right?"

Knowing he couldn't lie to his father and get away with it, Ben kept quiet.

"I am talking to you!" his father yelled.

Ben had to come up with a plan. Clearly, staying quiet was not helping matters. So, he decided to do as his father wised. "When I'm with the Tyler's," he said, "I do as I was told. I am dishonest with them in every way possible."

This was a true statement. Ben hadn't spoken a word of truth to either Kate or Gregorio. He had developed a false relationship with both of them.

"I see," Ednesto said with a smirk. "Well, I sure hope you keep up with those lies, as they are certainly necessary, especially if I want the Tyler's to fail task three—"

"What are you talking about?" Ben interrupted his father, a suspicious look crossing his face.

"You have no right to ask questions around here. I'm the boss, and I make the decisions around here. Are we clear?"

As Ben listened to his father's voice, he began shaking his head in frustration. The comments he had just heard were useless. Eventually, Ben nodded and apologized, realizing, at this point, that there was nothing else he could do. He decided to tolerate his father without protesting against him or attempting to change him. Ben sincerely believed that he was going through what he was going through was for the best. Unquestionably, there was a reason for it. Holding that in mind made him feel better—until his father spoke again.

"Son," Ednesto said, standing and walking over to the door. "Don't you know where you belong right now?"

Ben listened to a small creek outside. Looking his father straight in the eye, he shook his head in dismay. "You're kicking me out?"

"Yes, I am! I have every right to do so."

Nodding his head, Ben felt a certain tension come across him. He slowly whispered, "Yes, it's true. As the boss, you have every right to do so, although—" He paused, giving his father something to think about. "Although, since you're my father, it's different."

As Ben left the room, he was sure that he had planted a seed in his father's mind—one that would hopefully blossom and lead Ednesto to realize where he had gone wrong in raising his child. Ben felt that a huge burden had been lifted. He had finally told his father how he felt.

Chapter 22

As the moon lightened up the 'frozen' island, Kate tried hard to decode the mysterious sentence. As she focused her mind and concentrated only on the sentence, she felt her thoughts disturbed by something sudden and unexpected. As she lifted her head in wonder, she saw Ben approaching. She knew that something was wrong. Ben's eyes were red. As he drew closer, she noticed that they were also puffy. There was a tear at the corner of his mouth. Seeing this, Kate asked him what the problem was. *Is everything okay?* Kate thought to herself. Ben looked up at her but didn't answer. Her curiosity grew stronger. "*Ben, I don't understand what's going on. Are you okay?*" He was only able to shake his head. To him, this seemed the only option. Ben knew that there was no way possible for him to tell the Tyler's who he was and what had just happened. It had to stay a secret.

Frustrated by Ben's "silence", Kate got up. Just when she was about to let Ben know what she was thinking, he interrupted her thoughts and mumbled, "*It's nothing.*" Puzzled, Kate stared at Ben in wonder. Aware that on this island they were only able to communicate through their thoughts, Kate was usually able to read Ben's thoughts even if he tried to prevent her. Normally, on this island, Kate could access Ben's thoughts about his whole life—without his prior permission. But in this specific case, when Kate attempted to read Ben's mind, she was unable. Ben had realized that Kate had noticed something different about him and was hiding his thoughts behind a mental shield, of sorts. The shield gave him the power to ward off magic. Because the shield would remain in place only for an hour, Ben decided to use it to his advantage right now.

"*I know that something is up,*" Kate said as she sat back down on the ground, a confused look on her face.

"*No kidding. I have never acted this way. Well, I don't remember ever acting this way.*"

"*Seriously. I've only known you a few hours, but I'm positive that you have never acted this way. What's going on?*"

Silence. Ben couldn't tell her that he was her cousin. He couldn't tell her who his father was. Basically, he could tell her nothing. Much to her chagrin, Kate was clueless about Ben's life.

After a while, the young man figured that he had to say *something.* "*Uh, well, as you can see, I'm not myself.*"

"*Clearly,*" Kate said, interrupting him.

"*So, basically, the one and only reason for that is . . .*"

"*Is?*"

"*I'm really just not feeling well.*"

"*Oh,*" Kate said. She felt out of place, as though she were intruding in his life. Once that sensation came upon her, she decided that she better stop. In time, she sat down near the intriguing piece of paper. Wiping his puffy eyes, Ben knew that he couldn't maintain this false front, especially if he wanted to help the Tyler's. Since he was already in this situation, he should just make the best of it.

"*Let's look at what we do have,*" Ben said, sounding completely broken. Confused, Kate kept quiet as she waited for him to give a more detailed explanation. In response to her implicit request, he completed his thought: *"Let's try to figure out what is clear to our eyes."*

Understanding what he was asking, Kate clearly read the words in her mind. *"I am bigger than my friend."*

"Hmm," Kate said as she lightly placed a finger on her chin. *"I am bigger than my friend,"* she said again. *"This automatically means that there are two of them. Two of whatever the clue is talking about."*

"True. Friend is singular."

Feeling flattered, Kate felt herself blush before returning to analyzing the words on the paper. *"Two,"* she said, looking at the sky for inspiration. The dark sky began supporting numerous heavy clouds. Kate's eyes then shifted to the lake. She smiled while watching the obedient waters stream. This was the perfect place for inspiration. A person could develop their imagination here at Windermere Lake. Allowing her mind to wander off into the depths of the clouds, she thought about what they resembled. A bunny? A plane? A dinosaur? Feeling her brain loosen, she enjoyed the few moments of relaxation. Then something triggered her mind and began pulling her from her own little world. As she tried to follow it and tell it to stop, she slowly realized that it was Ben's loud thoughts. He was yelling at her, trying to pull her out of 'her world.' Slowly but surely, she abandoned her imaginary world and came back to reality. "*Sorry,*" she said shyly, her face flushed.

"*It looked like you were going to find your answer in those clouds or in that lake,*" Ben said derisively. His face began to take on color. Seeing this, Kate decided not to pay any attention to his smirk. She was just glad that he was wearing some expression, feeling that it was better to see something other than blankness on Ben's face.

"*I was actually hoping to,*" Kate said in the same mocking tone that Ben had just used.

"*Do you know how many things in this world come in pairs? 'Unconditional pairs' is your answer. There's no way you will find the answer. My—I mean, Ednesto is way too tricky.*"

"*Ben,*" Kate began, obviously not having listened to a word he just said.

"Yes?"

"Remember the first time we met, when you told my father and me that you were Ednesto's trusted advisor?"

Ben's forehead began to sweat. He suddenly felt pressure come upon him. For Kate to know the truth was the last thing he needed right now. As he got up and began pacing back and forth, he tried to calm himself. Then he replied. "Yes. I remember. Why are you bringing this up so suddenly?" Ben asked shakily while rubbing his hands against his pants, still trying to calm down.

"Well, since you said it yourself, you must know Ednesto very well. You know, like, his mentality, the way he thinks. Am I right?"

"Yes. Well, I guess."

"Perfect! So, can you help me out here, please? Knowing his mentality, you must know what pair he was thinking of, at least enough to guide me in the right direction."

"I know that he—"

"*Wait a second.*" Kate had interrupted. Ben grew more and more frightened. He heard suspicion in her voice, which began to worry him.

"*Yes?*" Ben asked, keeping his finger crossed as he inhaled loudly.

"*I just recalled another thing you told my father and me when we met.*"

"*What's that?*" Ben asked innocently, trying to remember what he had said and hoping that it was nothing that had accidentally slipped out of his mouth.

"*Yes, you said that you were the one who created all these tasks. You said that you were behind all this. Isn't that correct? Didn't you say that?*"

"*I did,*" Ben said, this time certain of his response.

"*My goodness, I can't believe that I didn't think of this earlier! You can help us! You're on our side now, aren't you?*" Kate asked, a hopeful gleam appearing in her large, dark eyes. Not knowing what to do, Ben felt that he should tell her the truth, although there was no way he could.

What Ben was going through now had taught him a very important lesson. He had always believed that honesty was the best policy, but he hadn't known that one cannot rationalize it by adding more lies to the first. Even a single lie eventually leads to other lies. Once a person chooses the wrong path, that of dishonesty, he or she will continue to hit hard bumps in the road and never feels good about any of his or her actions. The path of truth and honesty, however, was all good. This time, it was Ben's turn to learn a lesson. Leaving that thought aside, he looked at Kate as though waiting for her okay to continue speaking. Once Ben locked eyes with her, he picked up where he had left off.

"When I told you that I had created all three tasks, I was just, well . . . what I meant was that I had only created task one. You see, Ednesto has people working literally on every facet of his plan. So, I guess he chose me as the person to create task one. You understand?"

"Uh-huh, I see," Kate said, her face taking on a look of suspicion. As she gazed at Ben, she

knew that something was going on. For the first time, she was positive that he was lying to her.

Lies destroys lives, Kate thought to herself as she tightly held the special pen between her fingers. Aiming the light at the sentence, she tried to make out the words. She felt Ben blush. Ignoring her thought, he went to sit by her side and help. Minutes later, Kate removed her finger from the button and turned the light off. She placed it on the paper.

"Ben?" Kate asked, sounding frustrated.

"Kate, I don't understand what more you want to know. I already told you that—"

"It has nothing to do with you. Don't worry." The moment she said this, she sensed that Ben's bones had loosened and that he felt more at ease. She decided to go ahead with her question. *"I know this might sound weird,"* she began, *"but there is a certain question nagging my mind. I'm almost positive that you know the answer."*

"Go ahead," Ben said, feeling stressed.

"Well," Kate began confidently, *"I was wondering why Ednesto doesn't just kill us all."*

Seeing the expression on Ben's face, she quickly provided an explanation. "*If Ednesto is so evil, then why doesn't he just kill us all? Why does he have to make us suffer and perform the three tasks? I mean, if he wants my mom's powers, he should just force them out of her. Why are my father and I a part of it?*" Waiting for an answer, Kate gracefully got up from the rock she was sitting on. After a few long moments of silence, the atmosphere was thick. For the young girl until, finally, she heard Ben express his thoughts. Ben felt that it was time to tell Kate the truth, the real reason for the tasks.

"*When Ednesto established these three tasks, he was convinced that you would fail. As a matter of fact, he still believes this. Now, the only way he can get the powers is if you fail. Ednesto has no power to kill your mother while she retains the Murati powers.*" Ben paused dramatically. Kate's face showed puzzlement. "*I'm surprised that your father hadn't explained that to you. Anyway, it doesn't matter.*

Memory. Memory is something one cannot erase from another person's mind. If, G-d forbid, a person experiences a tragedy, then it will remain in their mind forever. Ednesto *thinks* that you will not be able to perform the tasks, which will eventually lead to the loss of your mother."

Seeing the broken look on Kate's face, Ben decided to intervene. He would hate it if Kate got hurt. "*To conclude, basically, Ednesto wants to hurt both you and your father—and, of course, also retrieve the powers from your mother.*"

After a long moment of silence, Kate slowly whispered, "*I know my mother. She will never give him the powers. Never.*"

Chapter 23

"Who understands children?" Ednesto said to himself as he gazed at the screen to see his son pacing around a rock. Kate watched him with hope in her eyes.

"They're so twisted. Everything they do, everything they say, never comes out clear. There's always something more behind it."

"That's true," a voice said, making Ednesto jump in fear. He turned around to find his advisor standing there. He smiled.

"I've got two beautiful children," Rango began, advancing towards his master. "Life became tough for us. Before long, my wife insisted on a divorce. I resisted as long as I could, but I finally gave in. Once I did, she was awarded full custody of the children. It's now been—" Rango paused as he looked up, searching. "Twelve years," he said, struggling to mask his sadness.

"I understand. It might be hard for you. Children are—"

"Children are what?" Rango bitterly yet with fear in his voice interrupted.

"I was just going to say how precious and important they are and that having a child is like bringing one's own heart into the world. It's like letting your heart walk the earth."

"Well, it sure doesn't seem like it," Rango replied in the same bitter tone as before.

"What are you talking about?" Ednesto said, surprised that Rango would speak to him so disrespectfully.

"You just said how children are precious and amazing, but the way you treat your only child makes it seem that you value children much less than you say you do . . ."

Feeling his face change color, Ednesto said through his teeth, "What I do with my child does not concern you. Now, *get out!*" Quickly facing the door, Rango ran for his life, fearing that Ednesto might pick up the first object in sight and throw it straight at him. As he quietly closed the door behind himself, Rango knew that he had given Ednesto something to think about. Setting aside the fear that Ednesto would fire him for his rude, albeit honest, behavior, Rango believed that Ednesto would act better the next time he was in his son's presence. Then again, he might not.

Throwing himself on the couch, Ednesto felt the pressure of being a father more than ever. His mind wandered to the time when he was told that he was going to be a father. The nine months of stress rushed through his mind. He remembered a lot about the difficult journey. Veronica was under a great deal of stress a one of them being her having very strong cravings for food. A slight smile appeared on Ednesto's face as he recalled frequently running to the store to purchase some ginger, as it was the only thing that eased his wife's nausea. As the months passed, it seemed an eternity to him. Waiting anxiously for a child to arrive and enhance their family wasn't easy on him. One rainy night, when Ednesto was in his study room finishing up some work, he felt his pager buzz.

Who is paging me at a time like this? He had thought, bending and looking at the pager to discover the identity of the mystery caller. Finally adjusting his eyes, he saw that his wife's cell phone number on the display. Quickly reaching for the phone, he dialed the number. As the phone rang, he felt hotter and hotter by the second. He thought that this must be it, as his wife was due in a week and a half. As he heard his wife's weak voice answer the phone, he held the receiver tight against his ear. Veronica was breathing loudly. She finally managed to speak a few words. Unsure that he had heard his wife correctly, he simply agreed. He ran out of the study and rushed into his house towards the stairs to his bedroom. Once there, he saw an empty bed. As he began feeling anxious, he wondered where his wife could be. Soon, he ran to the lower floor and out onto the front porch only to find an ambulance speeding away from the house.

Oh no! Ednesto thought to himself as he quickly ran back into the house to fetch his car keys. *She will never forgive me if I miss the delivery of our child.* Once in the car, he turned the key. The car's motor echoed throughout his sleeping neighborhood. Once out of the driveway, he made his way to the nearest hospital.

At last standing in front of the sliding doors, Ednesto walked in. At first, he saw a couple of men stretched out on couches, trying to get some sleep. Then, as his eyes shifted along the room, he noticed the front desk. Reaching it, he used the last breath he had to say, "Veronica Murati."

"Yes, she just arrived. She's on the fifth floor in room twenty-three. She—" Before the intake nurse was able to finish her sentence, Ednesto fled across the hall and stood impatiently at the elevator door. After a few seconds, he ran across the room towards the staircase, which he climbed to the fifth floor, where his wife was in labor. Once in the room, he saw his exhausted wife lying on the bed in agonizing pain. He went over to the side of her bed, crouched and quietly asked where the child was. As the room quieted, the staff members began looking at each other with confused looks on their faces. Immediately, Ednesto felt that he had said something wrong.

He remembered the doctor saying, "It doesn't take a few seconds for a child to enter this world. It's a long procedure." Puzzled, Ednesto left the room. He couldn't watch his wife in pain. As the sun shone the next morning, he heard a faint sound of a crying baby, which woke him up. As he followed the sound to find the child, he realized that he was entering Veronica's room. His wife, with an IV in her arm, lay on the hospital bed. Moments later, he noticed his child. Slowly walking towards his baby, he motioned to his wife to hold the child. Weakly, she stretched out her hands. Ednesto gracefully gathered the tiny child in his arms. He vowed never to forget that moment. He remembered the little brown eyes looking up at him, the perfect little nose, and the drawn lips. Everything seemed perfect. The thought of what kind of person this child would become occupied his mind more than ever. He never knew the truth about his little Ben—not until this very moment.

*   *   *

Rubbing his forehead in distress, Ben felt that he was failing at this task. He wasn't able to help the Tyler's the way he had wanted to. The young man definitely knew that he had the potential to help. Now, his inability to do so was causing him pain.

"We have to figure out what it says here, in the first part. Otherwise, there's no way we can figure out what the mystery pair is."

"True," Kate said as she nodded her head, willing herself to decode the phrase. Slowly, she focused her eyes on the first word that caught her eye. She thought that she might be able to figure out. "*Usually.* I'm positive that the 12th word is *usually.* I'm finally able to figure out more words."

"Well, that's amazing," Ben said, relieved. He pushed her to continue deciphering the words that would lead them to the next island, the second to last. Hopefully. They were *planning* to be done with the next two islands in the next half-hour, hopefully having enough time to finish the last task on time and thereby save Isabella. Kate didn't know where her mother was, but she was certain that it was in an awful place. If she had the opportunity to free her mother, she would take it, doing anything she had to in order to succeed. Finding herself daydreaming, Kate realized that Ben's eyes were desperately trying to get her attention, indicating that she was running out of time and must finish. Slightly nodding her head, she again set eyes on the mystery words.

"The fourth word looks like it's missing only one letter. Is it *right*? *Light? Bite?* No, the letter is swirled at the bottom. *Sight!* Yes, sight. Perfect! The second word is solved."

Feeling amazed and proud of Kate's determination in light of the difficult task, Ben felt helpless. Sensing that his knowledge was insufficient for the task, he just stood still, thinking warm thoughts to encourage her to continue. Setting a small smile on her face, Kate thought to herself, *if there's a will, there's a way.* "Clearly it has something to do with sight," she said, "although we don't yet know what until we determine the remaining words in the sentence."

"You're absolutely right, Kate. That's exactly what you should do. So, get back to work!"

Feeling shut down, Kate ignored Ben's comment. It was now most definitely not the time to pay attention to silliness. Soon enough, she returned to the little paper and continued brainstorming. "I can't believe I hadn't noticed these words earlier. Everything is finally so clear."

"Well, it's all about attitude. You have the capability to adopt a positive or negative mindset. Up to now, you have chosen a negative approach towards this whole situation. Luckily, you finally realized that it was time to change it. That's good."

Accepting Ben's rebuke, Kate smiled slightly while making it obvious that she was not the type of person who enjoyed being rebuked. Ben, understanding her meaning, lowered his eyes, somewhat ashamed.

"Okay, so, I figured it out," Kate said. After *usually* and *sight,* there's another word, right after *light. Sensitivity.* Wow, that was easy. I guess I just have to believe in myself."

"We should all know to do that. Anyways, with what I see right here, I think that this 'message' your uncle sent to us is not straightforward. It's a hint or a definition of some sort, and I guess this," Ben said as he pointed to the 'clear' writing beside the mystery sentence, "is what will actually help us find the answer."

Kate nodded her head, still focusing on the paper before her eyes. "I hear what you're saying. I also think that this may very well be a definition of some sort. Hopefully, I'll soon figure out what he's trying to tell us."

"Well, we don't need more words to figure out what it means. Clearly, you found the key word, *sight.* I don't know about you, but when I hear the word *sight,* I think of eyes—"

"That would make sense since eyes come in pairs, which speaks to the concept of 'I am bigger than my friend.'"

"It's scientifically proven that the right eye is larger than the left eye," Ben said. "Which brings us to conclusion that the next island will be the right one where we will receive our next clue to reach the last island—which will bring an end to task two."

As she nodded her head, Kate felt a huge burden lift and a happy sensation course through her body. She could finally move on. Quickly gathering her belongings, she motioned her father to the edge of the island where an orange canoe was awaiting them. All smiles, Ben, Kate, and Gregorio got into the boat to make their way to the next island. Unbeknownst to them, it the next island would present an obstacle that the three of them would fear themselves unable to overcome.

Chapter 24

Smiles were in the air, and happiness lay deep within them. As Ednesto watched the trio row towards their next island, he felt certain that the obstacle awaiting them there would impair their efforts to finish task three on time. Smiling, he turned to look at his four advisors, who were mirroring him. As Ednesto looked at them, he felt that evil was contagious. Whoever approached Ednesto was suddenly transformed. (Rango was an exception at times). Finishing up with tea, the five of them looked at each other in fascination. Torturing people, to them, was the greatest pleasure.

Looking down from the window at the maze they created, they felt like wise giants who knew it all. Up in the tower, everything was relaxed. Below, however, the Tyler's and Ben were tense and under pressure, a big question running through their minds: "How will we succeed this task?"

*   *   *

Feeling a bit 'lake-sick,' Kate lowered her head, hopeless. Then she felt a light tap on her back. Turning around with a grin, she saw her father smiling at her encouragingly.

"Don't you worry, child. We'll be able to overcome the obstacle waiting for us on this island, the same way we overcome all the others." As Kate smiled back at her father in gratitude, she felt that for an amnico patient, he sure knew a lot of things. She was operating under a misapprehension, though: Ben had written reminders on paper for Gregorio to look at whenever he felt confused. Ben. What a kind man. Kate felt so fortunate to have him with her even though she still remained suspicious.

"Ah, finally, to be able to talk, to have the power of speech again! On the island of silence, I finally understood what it was like to be mute. I guess I should be thankful for that. I will no longer take being able to speak for granted."

"Yes. I'm sure none of us will," Ben joked as he lowered his chin.

"Two more islands. Wow, this sure is exiting. I don't think I've ever looked forward to something as much as I look forward to this," Kate said, ignoring Ben's comment.

Suddenly, an image appeared in her mind. She felt a certain sensation rush through her bones and as though she was about to melt on the spot. The image grew and grew in her mind. Full of fright, the young girl yelled as she felt her head become heavier and heavier by the second, until it abruptly collapsed and fell onto her lap.

"No, no! This cannot be happening, please. No!" Kate repeated several times, almost in a whisper, as the canoe approached the second-to-last island. Desperately trying to get rid of the unpleasant thought, she began shaking her head and, once again, repeating the sentence. She was in denial of something. Momentarily, Ben's concerned look caught her attention. He was questioning if everything was all right with Kate. After a few moments of suspense, Kate just nodded her head, still in fear of the image before her eyes.

Could it be a vision? Kate thought to herself as she tried to distract herself from the horrific image. It was ghastly.

Kate saw her mother being beaten, her bruises getting darker and darker. What was happening to her mind? Why was it all of a sudden reacting so strangely? Kate had very little knowledge about magic and about her ancestry. The young girl felt adrenaline rush through her veins. The image kept returning to her.

"Kate, we have arrived. It's time to get out of the canoe," Ben said, trying to get her attention. Giving off the impression that she was unconscious, Kate buried her face in her hands.

Under her sweaty palms, her dark pupils swam in tears. Her body shook. Here they were at the island. For both Kate and Ben, this journey was one of never-ending trauma. For the first time, Kate was thankful that it was only for 11 hours.

Once on the island, Kate felt fortunate to have her father there. Even though he had amnico, she still felt the father-daughter connection between them. This taught her a life lesson: no matter the situation in which you find yourself, and no matter how hard you fall, the spark and light you experienced in the beginning remains. Going through this journey was definitely making Kate a stronger person, one who wouldn't come out the same as she went it.

Standing on the dull ground, Kate forced herself to forget the awful sight that lay deep in her imagination. It began vanishing but didn't leave completely, placing itself smoothly into a small corner of her mind. She didn't know when it would come back to haunt her.

"This island looks okay," Ben said as he tucked his hands into his pockets, looking around, as if searching for a specific object.

"Well, we never know with Ednesto," Kate said in a shaky voice, still traumatized.

"Everything might look okay on the surface, but if we get into the details, we'll find that it most certainly isn't okay."

"I guess you're right," Ben replied. As the trio walked along a path, they felt a sense of foreboding.

It was all over.

They would never make it.

Kate began to cry.

*   *   *

Dipping the perfectly beautiful feather into the placid black ink, Ednesto prepared to spill his thoughts. He reflected on how it all began.

> *Dearest Diary,*
> *I know I already spoke to you about this, but I can't help but mention it to you once again.*

He paused, bending over in the thick leather armchair as he inhaled sadness. Reaching over for the middle drawer, he opened it a crack. Tearing up, he leaned in to get a glimpse of the object inside, in the dark. Moments later, he had a small, wrinkled piece of paper tightly clutched between his fingers. He read it.

> *Ednesto Murati, born July 31, 1963.*
> *Dona Murati, died July 31, 1963*

Twenty-seven years later, when his father had died, Ednesto was left with this letter, which revealed the entire truth about who he was. He had never suspected a thing when his father remarried a young woman who easily passed for Ednesto's mom. His brother, who knew the truth, had always felt that Ednesto was the one to blame for their dear mother's death. Had he not have come to this world, then she never would have left it. In fact, a lot of things would be very different if Ednesto hadn't come to this world. There would be no family battle, no anger and, most important, no book . . .

When the truth was uncovered, Ednesto felt a certain anger towards his family. By being denied the right to know about his life, he was denied the right to live an honest life. He was convinced that his family's dishonesty had brought about agony and hardships that he was forced to endure his entire life.

Leaving that thought aside, Ednesto put the piece of paper back where it belonged. It would stay there for a few years, until he once again opened the drawer and once again felt that particular sadness overcome him. Taking the beautiful feathered quill out of the inkpot, he experienced a certain happiness, a feeling like no other. Expressing his feelings in words, in writing, in a diary, felt to him like an ancient practice. Perhaps one day, someone would find his diary and treasure it. More than once, people refrained from telling Ednesto that he wasn't living in the 18th century.

Smiling to himself, he gracefully and passionately wrote, grinning at the thought of the loss his niece would soon experience.

*   *   *

Their clothing torn apart and their faces dusty and soiled, the trio made their way onto the boat that awaited them at the end of the narrow island. Every island which they stepped foot on required one purpose. They had to make it to the other end of the island in one piece. Of course along the way solving riddles, which will lead them to know in what direction they should head. Each one of the islands had its own story its own fear she had to overcome, this island they were glad to be leaving. As predicted, the task was long and hard. Even though it was the shortest one they experienced, the pain and sorrow they felt made it seem much longer. Trying to dry the sweat from their bodies, they carried a sense of gratitude and joy as they approached the last island, which meant the end of task two. It became more and more difficult having an amnico patient for a partner. In addition to asking repetitive questions, once in a while Gregorio let out a terrifying shriek, waking the animals they had been desperately trying to avoid.

Looking down at her ripped garments, Kate tried to fix herself up, using safety pins she had luckily found in her backpack. Soon, the young girl lowered her head in dismay and misery. *Why is all of this happening to me?* She thought in silence, letting sadness flow through her body. Seeing her worried look, Ben looked at his torn shirt and tried to unravel Kate's feelings. Just when he was about to open his mouth and speak words of comfort, something caught his eye. He turned to look and saw a beautiful gold box sitting in the middle of the island. It appeared to be shining from within, even though they were on the midst of darkness. As Ben's jaw dropped in amazement, Kate lifted her head and beheld the same extravagant scene. In the next few minutes, they reached the last island. As fast as she was able to, Kate jumped off the canoe and raced towards the golden box, motioning for her father and Ben to follow her.

Having had enough of task two, she desperately wanted to finish it. The moment she stepped foot on that island, her entire body had become electrified. This was lightning.

She was lying on the ground when she heard a deep voice whisper, "Welcome to the end of the road."

Chapter 25

As chills crept up her back, Kate felt only partly conscious. The deep voice reverberated in her head. Again and again, she shook her head, trying to eliminate the thought that, to her, spelled destruction. The shade of Ben's facial skin changed to reflect the emotions that overtook him. He got Kate's attention just as his father stepped onto the island, while "un electrifying" the island for his presence. It was now Kate's turn to be confused. Seeing Ednesto rub Ben's back, force a grin and soon come walking towards her, Kate's heart beat dangerously fast. If just then a doctor checked her vital signs, she would be rushed to the hospital.

"Kate, dear, how is your mission going so far?" Ednesto paused and glanced at his watch. "With only two hours and fifteen minutes left?"

The adrenaline coursing through her body boosted Kate's energy. She straightened her back, lifted her chin and, to Ednesto's surprise, answered, "I'm fine. As a matter of fact, I'm passionately committed to completing this mission, as I did with the last one. How are you doing, Ednesto?" His nostrils flared and his eyes were piercing. He was enraged. Then, a dim smile began to appear on his tanned face. He had found the perfect way to hurt little Kate.

Heading back to his son, Ednesto hugged Ben tightly and said, in a loud enough voice, "I'm proud of you, Son. You did a great job fooling Kate and Gregorio throughout this whole mission." At that exact moment, the atmosphere thickened and Kate's pupils began swimming. Her cheeks blushed. Darker and darker they became until her face was red. Why was this happening to her? Her own cousin was betraying her, along with her evil uncle—all because of magic. Oh, how her body shivered when she thought of that word. Preoccupied with her thoughts, Kate slid to the ground in total dismay. She buried her face deep in her hands and then put her head between her knees. She wished she could just stay in that moment forever and forget about everything. Even though Kate's attitude was somewhat negative, deep inside she wished she had the ability to fix everything. But one word—a word that holds back many—was holding her back: *impossible.* How many people trap themselves by believing their situations to be impossible!

Kate's thoughts were interrupted by a loud cry. Suddenly shivering, she looked up in total fear. Embarrassed, Ben sat down beneath his father on the hard soil and said loud enough for Kate to hear, "Why are you doing this to me? I don't understand. You didn't have to—"

"One more word and I'll pound you to the floor until your soul leaves your body forever," Ednesto replied.

"Father, how could you be so evil? How is it possible that you want to destroy human life? Don't you know that human life is something to cherish, something that—"

"Enough!" Ednesto yelled, hoping to send shudders through everyone's body. "Didn't I say that I didn't want to hear another word come out of you? I thought I had made that clear. You filthy boy. No values, no values at all." He paused for a few minutes. Then, after gathering his thoughts, he resumed more gracefully, with a smirk across his face. "To answer your brainless yet obvious question requires a simple and logical explanation, with which I'm certain you're familiar: The only way I can retrieve Isabella's power is by killing her husband and daughter, of course." He paused as his son opened his mouth

to say something. Ednesto didn't allow him to speak. "But, why be so evil and make them got through this? Wasn't that your question, Son?" Noticing his son's faint nod, he stopped and reached for the small brown worn-out leather journal inside his long cape.

"This is the answer to all the questions you've asked me over the years," Ednesto said, moving from side to side to keep his cape from shifting and also to add to the drama.

The Evil Side. That was the book's title, which was printed in bright red on its cover. Once Kate and Ben caught sight of that book, they intuited that whatever was coming next would not be good. Ednesto began reading from the book's pages, which included sections on sorcery and black magic, replete with descriptions of the powers he hoped to receive. Moments later, he provided an answer to their question. The only way for Ednesto to get the Muratis' power was to kill all of the descendants of the oldest surviving child—who was, in this case, Isabella. "Of course, I can't just simply kill Kate. I have to prove to the wizard hierarchy that the Tyler's are unable to complete the mission I have entitled them to. Once that happens, the head wizards will hand the powers to the next-oldest survivor: *me.*"

Seeing absolute dread and terror in Kate's eyes, Ben couldn't help but begin to run over to comfort her with words of encouragement and support. Barely lifting his foot to balance himself, Ednesto reached out his hand and violently smacked Ben in the face. "Don't even think about it, Son."

"I have to," Ben said, furious.

Ednesto placed his right hand into his cape and brought out a shiny sword. Its sharpness scared Ben and Kate. "You take one more step, and this sword will not remain still."

"Really, Father? You would kill your own son? Your only son?" Ben asked, fear racing in his body.

"You know I would do anything for the power I desire," Ednesto replied without hesitation. He sneered. "One step, Son," he reminded Ben.

Then, Ben twisted his head towards Kate and slowly uttered,

"The song, Kate. Remember, you come from a Murati. You can—" In mid-sentence, Ben saw the sword fly into his arm.

He fell to the ground. Kate's cousin, her savior, her friend, lay there, wounded by his father. Completely disgusted, all Kate was able to do was grab her frightened father's hand and run, not only to get away but also to allow her insides the chance to unknot, her having just witnessed a terrible thing.

Kate kept flashing on the image of the dark red blood. She kept hearing her cousin's pain-filled screams after he had just been extremely hurt.

"So, I guess it's time for you to finish your task. Bad luck," Ednesto said, smiling evilly and dramatically twirling his cape. He fled to a large boat awaiting him at the edge of the island.

Kate decided to move on and concentrate on the thing that affected her most: finding her mother.

"The song, Kate. Remember, you come from a Murati. You can—"

Those words came back to her again and again. What song? Whatever song it was, it was clearly the key to getting to the gold box and unlocking the clue for the third and final task. Kate wept until her eyelids lifted with a sudden emotion.

She remembered.

Finally.

Soon, she began humming the tune that brought back hundreds of childhood memories. Moments later, she sang the lyrics. "When it's hard, when life seems to turn its back . . ." She inhaled profoundly and grabbed her father's hand, continuing to sing. "Don't give up. Just continue and turn to the right." Doing as the lyrics commanded, Kate obediently turned to the right, where the ground sloped to protect her from the electrified wires. Feeling sure that she had a chance of making it out alive, she sang louder, calculating each one of her steps. "And remember not to let go of the sack. Jump three times, like you're flying a kite." Tightly clutching her backpack, she jumped high three times, noticing sharp knives rising from the muddy ground beneath her.

"Then close your eyes, as though you're in a windy desert. Then, roll on the ground, for a better view of the stars."

Cobras swung from the trees! Kate rolled on the ground until she came to the song's last directive: "After that, slowly get up and button your coat so you don't get hurt. Then, run to left, and live your life as passing cars."

A thick layer of acid began spreading across the island. Once Kate quickly ran to the left, she realized that she was saved. Rescued! Lifting her eyes to the sky above, she slowly whispered, "Thank you, G-d."

There it was. The beautiful gold box sat there mirroring her. She placed her hands on it, her thumbs in the center, and tried to lift the lid. It was locked.

"What now?" she whispered to herself as she flung her hands in the air, totally discouraged.

"Kate, I know very little of you and your family troubles, although I have learned quite a bit in the past hour. One thing I am positive about is that you should most certainly *not* give up. Give yourself a chance. You know you're able to."

Listening to her father speak to her, Kate felt her heart warming. Momentarily, her frown turned upside down as she began thinking. She paced and studied the box until she realized that a key wasn't required to open it. It seemed to open on an audio cue, she determined. So it happened that Kate began saying things in quick succession. Each time she said something incorrect, she heard a piercing sound come from the box.

"Murati, Ednesto, power, hate, evilness . . ." The longer she stood before the box, the stranger her words became.

"Grass, duck, bird, eyes . . ." Kate felt that this was the most difficult part of the task. All the other times, she knew she would be able to succeed because there had been an end point to the tasks. But now, she didn't even know in which direction to head.

Sitting on the ground, Kate tied her long hair into a high ponytail and then began rubbing her hands in distress. Then she felt something on her middle finger.

"Mom, how could I forget?" she said as she froze in place, hoping to divine the words to open the box. Quickly removing the ring from her finger, she peered inside the box to find a word shining at the bottom.

Excitedly jumping to her feet, Kate stood before box and gently articulated, "Lucky 11."

Chapter 26

Hot tears stung her eyes as the lid to the gold box flew open, accompanied by a strong light. It was so powerful that Kate felt blinded. She lowered her head. Kate's feelings were mixed. Was she feeling happiness, excitement or, perhaps, fear?

Trying to ignore her thoughts, Kate now felt that it was now important to live in the moment. Minutes passed and the light began to dim. Soon enough, she could look at it. Both she and Gregorio looked up, finally able to discover what was inside the golden box. Digging her hand deep inside it, Kate's fingers felt a piece of parchment. She shivered.

This is it! She thought to herself. *Finally, the last task. I'm on my way, Mom.* With all her sorrow and pain, she had still managed to smile a little as she turned to look at her confused father. *How can this day get any worse?* Kate thought to herself. Just as she retrieved the paper from the box, she felt spooked, as if she had just received an answer to her question. The shiny letters, neatly printed on the white piece of paper, stood out, thanks to the paper's reflective gold border. Without further ado, Kate wiped away a tear, which she hoped would be the last, and began reading about the short but murderous mission she would have to complete.

Slowly placing the paper tightly between her sweaty fingers, she inhaled deeply, hoping that the task wouldn't be as difficult as she was expecting it to be. She was disappointed.

"I'm placed in a dark, hollow place—a vacant land, a land with ice . . . No one can pronounce my 16-letter name," the paper read.

Confused, Kate reread the paper 15 times and, along the way, explained to her father what was happening.

Her pupils began to swim. Moments later, as if showered by magic, she received a vision. Kate concluded that she was actually getting somewhere. Speaking her thoughts, she said, "A dark place. Okay. So, this means it's neither in the city nor in the country. It's a place infrequently inhabited by people—yes, since here it mentions a hollow, vacant land. Okay, so we at least know one thing." She paused and looked to the right, wondering where that place might be. She shrugged her shoulders and carried on with her monologue.

"A land with ice? Where can that be? Alaska?"

Glancing at her watch, Kate quickly made the connection that with two hours left; she and her father had no time to fly to Canada. Then, her eyebrows lifted, her frown faded and, most important, her cheeks became rosy. "Iceland! How could I not think of that?" she said, looking at her father. She dug her hand into her backpack and retrieved her Blackberry before realizing that there was no Wi-Fi. She pushed the smartphone back into her backpack and exhaled.

A 16-letter word? Where in the world is a place with 16 letters in its name?

A deep voice broke the thick silence. "Instead of wasting our time here, what about we get on the plane and hopefully find someone who can help us?" Gregorio offered.

Surprised yet thankful, Kate followed her father's advice. She unlocked the second part of the box by speaking the word *Iceland.* Kate excitedly removed the two plane tickets.

Their destination was 1,760 kilometers from London and with the new airplane THW Turbo Concorde that travels as fast as 1320 km/H it will take them 1 hour and 20 min to get there.

After a 10-minute cab ride from Windermere, Kate and Gregorio arrived at the airport. The plane took off shortly thereafter. Their flight seemed long, like a journey overseas, although in reality it was just a jaunt.

Only once she was on the plane did it hit Kate. How could they possibly be going to Iceland when their next task would have to do with fire? "I hope this isn't one of his vicious schemes," she quietly whispered to herself, shedding warm tears.

At that moment, a flight attendant was in the center aisle checking on the passengers. Noticing the tears on Kate's cheeks, she offered to help. Gladly accepting, Kate followed her to a section of the plane where the staff took their breaks. Kate followed the tall, dark-haired woman down the aisle, noticing her long, wavy hair and her tidy navy blazer nicely fitted onto her slim body.

"So, dear, tell me. What's going on?" the flight attendant said in a sweet voice surprisingly absent a British accent. Usually, Kate kept her personal life to herself, but she felt that there was something special about this flight attendant. She felt a certain connection to her. So, Kate began spilling her feelings to this stranger. They spoke for quite a while, with Kate telling her about practically everything she had been through: her struggle with her father's amnico, her pain about her kidnapped mother, her evil uncle and, most important, how she was an 11-year-old without the experience to carry such a tremendous burden on her tender back. At one point, the flight attendant cut off a teary-eyed Kate in mid-sentence.

"You said that your father had amnico. Is that correct?" the kind flight attendant asked with a warm, pitying smile.

"Yes," Kate mumbled through her tears.

"Well, then, I have some good news for you," the woman said jollily.

"*Good*. What a word," Kate said to herself, loud enough for the flight attendant to hear.

"Don't say that, dear. Life has so much to offer. If only you delve into its beauty, you will be able to find more than you desire."

As though the flight attendant had said nothing, Kate continued her thought. "*Good.* That word isn't even in my vocabulary," she said, this time sobbing.

"Perhaps, but it's in your eyes," the kind woman answered. Kate remained silent for a few moments, giving the flight attendant the opportunity to speak.

She began. "Since I am a stewardess, I am familiar with the world. I have traveled practically from one end of the globe to the other. On my many journeys, which were also adventures, I was exposed to and learned quite a few things. One thing I discovered was a plant named Rivry. Whoever ingests this plant is cured of amnico in just seconds. Kate's eyes lit up with joy! The flight attendant saw the excitement in the young girl's eyes and continued talking about the 'magic' plant. For the first time, it did not bother Kate, not even a bit, to hear the word *magic.* After excusing herself for a minute, the flight attendant returned with a small black leather box with camel trim. It was sleek and looked beautiful—although not as beautiful as what was inside. With a lovely dimpled smile, the flight attendant opened the box, not shifting her gaze from Kate's shining eyes. Kate, excited, gasped as she beheld the bright yellow and purple flower inside the box, its petals shining against the box's striking red lining.

"My brother suffered from the same thing years ago," the flight attendant said.

"Is this really—" Kate said.

"The flower that cures amnico? It sure is!"

Joy lit Kate's face. Anxious to cure her father, she began pacing the small space where she stood with the flight attendant. After a few short moments, the kind flight attendant handed Kate a cup with a light pink liquid inside. It was the flower's essence.

A bit later, Kate was by her father's side, pressuring him to down the drink. She succeeded. Soon, her father fell into a deep sleep. She waited a while for him to wake, but he didn't. So, Kate went to speak with the kind woman who had helped her out.

The flight attendant asked where Kate and her father were heading.

Ashamed but not without dignity, Kate answered, "I don't know . . ."

Wearing a kind smile, the flight attendant placed her hand on Kate's left shoulder and slowly whispered, "Let me hear the clue." A surprised look shortly appeared on Kate's face. Then, she began reading the crinkled piece of paper. When she was finished, the beautiful flight attendant flashed a striking smile and said in heavenly, soft voice, "Eyjafjallajökull."

"What?"

"Eyjafjallajökull," she repeated, this time elaborating. "It's one of the smaller icecaps of Iceland, situated to the north of Skógar and to the west of Mýrdalsjökull. The icecap covers the caldera of a volcano with a summit elevation of 1,666 metres. This volcano has erupted relatively frequently since the last glacial period, most recently in 2010."

With that information, Kate felt thankful to understand, yet frightened to know the reality. With 10 minutes left until the plane would land, the passengers buckled their seat belts. The aircraft began to shake. Kate quickly thanked the kind flight attendant and then returned to her seat. Fearing the worst, and knowing Ednesto, Kate clutched her hands tightly around the armrests. As she closed her eyes, she felt a warm hand surround hers. A familiar voice slowly whispered, "It'll be okay."

Chapter 27

❧ • ❧

The moment they stepped foot on land, Kate and Gregorio noticed a dark mountain not too far in the distance. Shivers crept up their spines. They felt frightened.

"Kate, dear," her father said kindly, "you really have nothing to worry about. This is our last task. Hopefully, we will be able to overcome the terrible things it has to offer and have Mother back with us once again. The only way Ednesto will be able to kill us is if we fail this task."

He paused, smiling slightly, and then resumed, certain that he had his daughter's complete attention. "We know that that's the only way he will be able to destroy us, just as it is written in the book."

Seeing her father be himself made Kate happy. Just being in her father's presence lifted her spirits. She cared about nothing else at the moment. Family was a concept that continuously invaded her thoughts. One may be the wealthiest, most respected person alive, yet if he or she lacks family, then those other things are worth nothing.

The cold began to penetrate Kate's stiff bones, seemingly trying to unlock an emotion trapped therein—fear, perhaps, or maybe anxiety. Kate and Gregorio walked through the wide, deserted land towards the mountain whose identity remained unknown to them. Dark colors blending with the cold air made the atmosphere seem frightening. Rubbing her hands together and trying to avoid the cold, Kate noticed a golden box placed neatly in the middle of a deep icecap. Quickly grabbing her father's arm, she ran towards it, slipping a few times in the process. Once there, Gregorio pushed Kate behind himself. As though taking charge, he inhaled deeply and ran his cold hand against the box. Then he flung it open. This time, red light shone from the box, which played dramatic classical music. Next, Gregorio removed a white envelope. This is what the paper inside read:

> With half an hour left, there isn't much you can do.
> With half an hour left, you have to finish this task.
> Eyjafjallajökull is not a mountain.

Eyjafjallajökull is something much worse.

Tucking the paper into his left pocket, Gregorio knew exactly what that mountain was. Seeing her father shake in fear, Kate began to understand what this task was all about. She wasn't sure if she wanted to finish it. She knew that climbing this mountain would put her life in danger. It definitely wasn't the ideal thing to do, yet she knew that it was ideal to save her precious mother, whom—if Kate succeeded— she would see again in half an hour. Everything depended on Kate now. She knew that she had the power to succeed as well as the power to fail. A greater power was now in her hand, Kate realized: the power of choice. Anyone can claim the power of choice and use it either negatively and positively, depending on the person. Very fearful, Kate followed her heart and began to walk behind her nervous father after quickly digging her sweaty palm into her father's heavy satchel to retrieve an item she hadn't seen in quite a while. The golden horn lit the dark land she stood on and also lightened her spirits. She felt as if she had received a warm hug from her mother. With such a sentiment within her, she decided to check on the music box. As she gently placed her ears beside it she was unable to hear it so clearly as fear overcame her she quickly pressed it against her cheek to discover the instrument play very slowly. She once again felt her mothers hug. Now what she feared most was what the hug meant. Was it to encourage her or to comfort her in the midst of something tragic? Throwing that thought aside, Kate smoothly placed the mysterious horn back into her father's satchel.

"Wait up, Dad," she called from behind her father while running. Seeing his daughter struggle and cry, Gregorio stopped and impatiently waited for her to catch up. Once Kate was beside her father, he bent over to speak to her. Now completely relaxed, he looked deep into her eyes and, inhaling profoundly, kneeled before her, slowly whispering to his beautiful daughter.

"We have to stop surviving. Instead, we should start living," he said. The moment Kate heard those words, they struck her deep in the heart. She realized that the saying was true: life is not measured by the number of breaths we take but by the moments that take our breath away. Analyzing that thought gave her a completely different understanding of the objectives of this mission. She got to her knees and tied her boots. Then she jumped up, ready to proceed. Gregorio nodded, slowly zipped his hooded jacket, and grabbed Kate's hand to run towards their destiny.

Hiking had never been Kate's cup of tea. She didn't enjoy climbing and jumping. However, given the strong power which lay deep within her, she believed she would succeed. It all started with one step. Anything a person wants to do and succeed at starts with one step. One just has to begin, and then the rest will come. Kate kept that in mind, along with the idea that it's not for her to finish. That is what she held in mind every step she took up that mountain. So it was, step after step, she and her father ascended the tall, pointy mountain. Every five minutes or so, they felt the need to stop and regain some strength before continuing (and finishing in one piece, Kate hoped).

"Can I please have some of that hot water you packed for us?" Kate breathlessly asked her father as she sat down on a rock. Seeing the despair in his daughter's eyes, Gregorio put down his heavy sack and opened it to retrieve the water bottle for his daughter. A frown appeared on his face as he dug his hand deeper into the satchel. Then, searching his pockets for what seemed like rescue, he found nothing. He was in complete dismay. His first thought was, *how will we ever be able to climb this volcano if we have no hot water?*

Just then, he had a thought. "Wait right here, darling, while I retrace our steps to see if the water bottle slipped out as we were walking." He paused for a few moments to collect his mixed emotions. "Stay right here. The last thing we need right now is for you to get lost." This time, the tone of his voice had raised five octaves. This was not the father Kate once knew, the kind father who encouraged her and taught her that nothing could or would tear her down. Still, Kate obeyed her father, believing that she owed him respect.

After Gregorio walked off, Kate was left with her fearsome feelings about the dark volcano. After a bit, when her father still hadn't returned and the knots in her stomach grew tighter and tighter, she felt lonely, as though abandoned. Still, she had the energy and strength to follow her heart and do what it desired. She was extremely curious about that golden horn and wanted to know its story. After walking over to her father's satchel, Kate slowly looked over her shoulder twice. She was nervous that her father might be watching. It seemed that the coast was clear, however. This was her moment.

As she gently placed her hand into the warm bag, she felt her father's everyday items before she felt the horn. Adrenaline rushed through her veins. She slid her hand from one end of the horn to the other, her excitement rising. Feeling that it was safer to stick her head in the satchel than to take the object out, she put her head in the satchel. Her face reddened in pain. The horn's golden surface was so smooth and shiny. She removed her hand. Admiring the horn's stunning yet understated beauty, Kate thought that she should stop, since she heard her father's loud footsteps somewhere behind her. She slowly removed her hand from the beautiful object. She looked at it one last time, convinced that she wouldn't have another chance to see it. She missed it already. As Kate closed the satchel, she felt that she had switched off a light that was both physical and spiritual. She felt as if the light had spoken to her heart.

"What are you looking for?" Gregorio, breathless, asked from behind her. Kate jumped in fright, quickly placed the bag on the rocky soil, and turned to find a steamy bottle in her father's hand (which they received from the kind stewardess).

"Oh, you frightened me," she said as she approached her father.

"Well, I hope you haven't touched any of my stuff," he said coldly, signaling Kate to take a step back and handing her the small cup of water. Staring at her father, Kate sipped it gingerly yet it still managed to burn her tongue.

Resuming their journey, Kate and her father walked, climbed and hiked in pain and agony. After some time, Kate felt as though the sweat on her forehead had turned to ice. The cold was nearly unbearable. Kate felt that her agony would last forever. In addition, she was concerned about her father's stern attitude, hoping that it was just a phase. Her cold, bare hands stiffened with each step she took. She felt a feeling she couldn't describe, a pain similar to having a splinter, which feels buried deep in the skin even though it barely pierces the surface. In addition, Kate felt stress and the effects of adrenaline. Her fingers felt as if they might fall off.

Seeing his daughter in distress and hearing her exhale loudly, Gregorio turned to see if everything was okay. Still in his 'serious' mode, he decided to keep quiet. Kate felt her heart break. She shuddered in despair. Slowly removing one of her hands from the icy volcano, she put herself in danger. Her father had tried to warn her, but it was too late. There she was hanging from a volcano with one hand. The unbelievable reason? Because she *needed* to check the time to see if she was too far behind to save her mother.

"Grab the mountain. Do it this instant!" Gregorio said urgently.

Since her hand was already off the dangerous mountain, Kate figured that she could achieve one last thing. *How much good can a second really do? What can happen in a second?* She thought to herself. She wasn't aware that practically anything could happen in a second, until she had entered this task.

Kate remembered a story she had once heard: A man was trying to explain to his friend that God runs the world and that everything is up to Him. So, he told him, "You know, if God wants to, He can take away all your money in one second."

Laughing, the other man looked up sheepishly and said, "That's impossible. I have millions of dollars spread across many world banks. All the banks in the world can't just disappear in one second."

Grinning, his friend said, "Yes, that is true—although *you* can disappear in one second. Your life can be taken from you in just one second."

When Kate looked down, she saw her feet dangling. This was the thought that appeared in her mind . . .

Chapter 28

Kate couldn't reach the mountain with her free hand. She wondered if this was because she couldn't see a place to grab onto or if her arm simply couldn't stretch that far. She felt as though she was inside of an illusion. She also felt crazy. Here she was confronting her worst fear: of heights. She saw no way to overcome it, not even with the help of the most talented therapist in the world. It seemed to her to be a lost cause. The fear in her father's eyes remained, as if frozen. Yet Kate was certain that her father's fear was not merely frozen in place. It was alive as he strained to observe her every move. As she watched her father, Kate felt determined to do what she *had* to. It was a *need*, not a *want*, and so she once again attempted to reach out. Her father let out a yell, pleading. Kate turned her face away. Grinning, she nodded in disagreement. There she was dangling from a mountain by two numb fingers, heartbroken that her father didn't trust. After twenty seconds, which seemed to last for a lifetime, Kate dug her free hand into her backpack (which was placed on her right which somewhat made it easy for her to reach.) to retrieve the object that would soon reveal the secret she desperately yearned to divulge. She felt the beautiful music box. Its sounds reached her ear as she lifted its lid, afraid of dropping it and even more afraid of letting go of the mountain. Once heard the music, she was satisfied. She gently caressed it, giving her body a little push to hug the volcano. Letting out an enormous sigh, her father continued hiking after seeing that all Kate had wanted was to learn if her mother was still breathing, still alive.

*   *   *

A continuous clicking sound plagued Isabella's weak mind. Shaking her head in annoyance, she breathlessly yet forcefully said through her teeth, "Please, Ednesto, turn off that obnoxious sound. It is the last thing I want to put up with right now."

Turning his head towards his niece, Ednesto wore a slight, cruel, mocking grin on his dark face as he continued disturbing the frail, pained woman sitting a few feet behind him. Although he had ignored her, Isabella asked him again to cease making the racket. "Do us both a favor and stop making that awful sound, please!" she begged, anxiety in her eyes as she cried uninvited tears. As the long minutes passed, she couldn't help but restate her desire that he quit engaging in this senseless behavior and put an end to the clicking noise, whatever it was. Isabella then slowly shifted her head to the right to discern what was causing the sound. There he was clicking away, playing Solitaire on the computer he had just bought on the way to Iceland. Still ignoring her, Ednesto grinned as he carried on. On the side of his screen was a small window showing live feed of the Tyler family as they undertook the third task. The sight of them entered deep into Isabella's heart as she awaited rescue. Eventually, Ednesto broke the silence by letting out a simple laugh in reference to what he was watching on his screen. He was in the habit of putting down the Tyler's as though it were an enjoyable sport. Watching Kate and Gregorio fail, watching pain dig deep holes in their hearts, seemed to have planted a seed of happiness in his heart.

Trying to get a better view of her family's struggles, Isabella craned her neck, brushing away some strands of hair from her face. As she lowered her chin to the right, trying to use it to remove the hair from her eyes she fell to the ground. Because her hands were tied with thick rope, she was unable to break her fall. It seemed to Isabella that her uncle hadn't even noticed her fall, as he just sat there clicking away at Solitaire. As she began to sob in distress, it came to Isabella's attention that Ednesto had finally noticed her. He looked at her with hatred. She was certain that he would leave her lying on the cold floor. To her surprise, he quickly called for one of his advisors to lift her chair and bring it closer to him, but not too close—as maintaining his distance continued showing Isabella who was boss. The torture began. Isabella was seated near Ednesto's computer, where she watched her family on the screen. She still felt as if she were living the moment with them. She felt that she was to blame for their fear, stress and pain. If it wasn't for her, if she hadn't received the powers, then she wouldn't have this great burden to carry—nor would her husband and daughter have been forced to embark on this risky journey. As she observed them, she felt their agony and stress. Each step they took resulted in another blunder. If one of them tripped, Isabella felt it, too. Turning her head away, she refused to keep watching her family fail in their efforts to save her. The mere thought that they wouldn't come out of this alive made Isabella sick. Seeing the smile on Ednesto's face widen, Isabella didn't have the emotional strength to look at him too long. Resting above Ednesto's desk was a clock.

Isabella stared at the second hand as it ticked and marked the passage of time. Isabella felt that this was never going to end, that she was stuck in this moment forever.

Trying to hide the fact that she could no longer watch her family struggle, Isabella lifted her head and took in everything she saw. The room she was in was beautiful. She pretended to admire the thick turquoise drapes brushing the exquisite marble floor. The wide, crystal-clear window made her feel as if she were actually standing on the icy volcano. Scanning the room, Isabella kept her eyes off her family as though memorizing each finely designed detail. Even though she had recently experienced torture and had been forced to stay in a dungeon, she found herself smiling. She felt fortunate that G-d was showing her kindness for at least her family was still alive. The pleasant moment was interrupted by an unpleasant sound.

The chuckle. How she hated to hear that sound come out of Ednesto's thin lips. Isabella felt just then that she would simply be unable to withstand the test, unable to witness her family's determination as they persevered through the treacherous mission. Ednesto slowly tuned his head, making eye contact with Isabella. For the split second their eyes were locked, he insinuated with a look that the end would not be pretty. She burst into uncontrollable tears. Ednesto felt joyous, not only because he had hurt his niece, but also because he was pleased to have hurt someone else much more deeply.

*   *   *

Kate felt fear and anxiety. She wasn't sure where its source was, but she was convinced that her mother was with her in spirit, every step of the way. Finally able to see the volcano's peak from where she was standing, Kate felt that it was the light at the end of the tunnel. It seemed to her that she and her father had found their fate, that their destiny was now revealed. Just seeing that peak, seeing the end of the arduous journey, gave her a boost, evident that by them reaching the peak will bring their journey to an end, no explanations were needed whatsoever by Ednesto. Even though she was extremely fatigued and her body was cramped, the fresh air and movement did her good. Amazingly, she did not question why or how she suddenly felt better. It seemed that every breath she took was accompanied by sparks. Recalling other pleasant sensations she experienced in the last 10-plus hours of her life, she then found herself facing the fact of her betrayal at the hands of her great-uncle. At this point, she became sad, realizing the horror.

Kate abruptly fell back 10 feet. Although the peak remained in view, the distance seemed too large for her to cross. The mountain's size grew every second. The more she tried to climb to the top, the more impossible it seemed. Yes, the feeling had returned. Allowing a steam of tears to wet her cheeks, which were rosy from the unbearable cold, all that concerned Kate at the present time was finding a place to plant her feet. She had no firm ground upon which to stand. However, as usual, she decided to focus on the bright side of her situation. Her father was once again mentally present. She was entrusted with power, which was a plus. Of course, she wouldn't expect anyone else to understand the joy that now warmed her broken heart. She would expect people to understand the pain in her soul.

Kate recalled a favorite saying and decided to plant it as a seed into her now experienced and wiser mind: "When things get tough and you wonder where G-d is, remember that a teacher must always keep quiet during a test."

This was her test, one she desperately desired to pass. As mixed feelings blossomed in her mind, Kate's thoughts were suddenly interrupted by a growl.

As she looked down in wonder, she noticed the land beneath her rumble. Could this be the end?

Chapter 29

❧ • ❧

Moving her head in all directions, Kate tried to deny the fact that the mountain had just shook. The dangerous part of this mission had just become apparent, and Kate was afraid. The last thing she needed was for the volcano to wake up.

"Daddy, what do we do?" she desperately asked her father, her face flushed.

"Oh, I was hoping that you hadn't notice the movement," he replied.

Not answering her worried father in words, Kate shifted her eyes as though asking, how long will this last? Understanding her discreetly delivered message, Gregorio gave a wise answer. "According to my knowledge, a volcano lets out a signal about 57 minutes before it erupts."

He paused then, gripping the rocky volcano. He realized that his life was in the hands of this rocky mountain. Gregorio felt that he was standing in the middle of a ball of fire. Bright orange and red flames flashed in his mind as he wandered deeper into his thoughts. The room he imagined himself in was spacious, but its perfect arrangement made it seem terribly creepy. The swirls, the lights, the mixture of colors and the sounds made him feel miserable, as though he were standing in the middle of a clock as its hands moved from number to number and pleading for it to halt, even for just a minute. Feeling his mind race in circles, all he wanted to do was remain stable and keep his head from hitting the ground. In complete desperation, he let out a sigh, shaking his head in denial. He was overwhelmed with frustration, anger and fear—but also by love. Love for his dear, valuable family, for his wife, for his daughter who would probably not live to see another day. *No,* he thought to himself, *I will not surrender. I will not lose hope.* Life is full of challenges. The one who overcomes them is the true hero. The one who conquers his or her natural instincts is the true hero. Once more, Gregorio glanced at his watch, this time full of strength, power and hope. His head held high, he continued climbing the volcano. Kate followed. Suddenly, a scream made his heart stop. He abruptly turned his head and saw his daughter hanging from a rock. His first instinct was to reach out a hand and to his beloved, terrified daughter. How many times had the end of the road appeared to him? How many more times would he have to suffer? How many more times would he have to confront the image of the end of their lives? Struggling to push those thoughts aside, he realized that he had to do something different if he was to get his daughter back to safety.

"Please, Kate, don't give up. You can do it."

The image of the clock appeared before his eyes once again. As the second hand moved, he *knew* that he and Kate would never make it unless they overcame their negative emotions and let their willpower outshine all impediments. With anxiety and determination, Gregorio knew that he could master his destructive side.

"Help, I can't reach. *Daddy,* please!" On the deserted volcano, all he heard was the dreadful terror in Kate's pleading voice. Heartbroken, Gregorio could do nothing but stare.

"Here, take my hand!" he said, crying. His tears soon became cold and icy. Annoyed, the 'responsible adult' attempted to control the situation. He looked at his clothes to determine if something he was wearing could be turned into a makeshift rope that his daughter could hold onto. No article of clothing he wore would do, though. Giving Kate a sorrowful yet resentful look, he found no words to express the emptiness in his heart. Not being able to help his daughter in her moment of need crushed him. Just then, he spotted the scarf wrapped around Kate's neck.

"The scarf! Hurry! The scarf!" The clock was ticking. The actions he took in the next second would determine whether Kate lived or died. In pain and anger, Kate found no way to remove the beautiful turquoise silk scarf and toss it to her anxious father. Hearing him whisper, Kate pleaded with her eyes for her father to raise his voice and let her hear what he was saying again and again. Gregorio comprehended her message and did as she wished.

"It's not for you to finish," he said. As those words echoed in her head, Kate wanted to know what it meant and why it brought back memories.

"It's not for you to finish." As those words swirled in her mind, as if trying to haunt her,

Kate was still unable to discern the meaning of the phrase. Then it hit her: it was the saying she heard when she was younger, before she fell asleep each night. Kate remembered reading that a child's self-esteem is built between birth and 11 months of age. With parental love, devotion, care and appreciation, a child's foundation is developed during that brief span of time. With all the attention Kate's parents had given to her, this phrase had come up—and not just once. A child who knows that he or she is the best thing in his or her parents' eyes grows up with a bulletproof vest and knows that he or she has the capability to overcome any obstacle later in life.

Having remembered warm moments from her childhood, Kate decided to alter her frame of mind. *It all begins with a simple step,* she thought. If she just gives it her time, effort and strength, she will achieve her goal. As if she had just received a fiery boost, she unwound the scarf from her frozen neck and, with all her strength and determination, threw it into the air, hoping that her father would be able to catch it. As it flew, she prayed that her father would soon hold the silky scarf in his frigid hand. She watched the turquoise fabric sail in front of the clouds, as if it were in slow motion. The scarf looked like a beautiful butterfly emerging from a cocoon.

The butterfly. How the insect fascinated Kate. A question she often considered was why G-d made the caterpillar to go through so much pain and so many hardships. Why hadn't He just created the butterfly as its own creature? A lecture she had heard had helped her understand. When a person yearns to become better, he or she must go through a painful series of hardships and suffering—just like the caterpillar does before transforming into the most beautiful insect. In times of sorrow and sadness, Kate tried to be like the butterfly: after resting in darkness, she would change. Interrupting Kate's thoughts, Gregorio spoke loudly.

"Clutch the scarf tightly! We have no time. Hurry!"

Turning her head from side to side, Kate felt adrenaline overtake her body. Straightening her legs, she prepared to catch that scarf and help save her own life. Letting her fingers sway from side to side, she struggled to grasp it. She had to if she wanted for her life to continue, if she wanted to save her mother from that awful prison.

Stretching her hand to the utmost extent, Kate began thinking back to more pleasant times.

*   *   *

Grinning widely, Isabella felt good about her family. Her dear husband was finally normal again, conscious and aware of his life and his goal for this horrible mission. Thanks to the help of a mysterious stranger, his previously lost identity had now been returned. Having placed a hidden camera on Kate herself the duo were able to watch even the most minor detail which occurred throughout their journey. Shifting her head Isabella began observing the beautiful room, which all of a sudden seemed shallow and empty, she felt the anxiety and fear her daughter was going through. She couldn't physically comfort her daughter, but she could provide emotional support from a distance. Whatever she was able to give, she gave. After all, all she wanted as a mother was to please her child. Indulging her feelings in the dark, Isabella yearned to pass on her hopes and dreams for her daughter. As her mind wandered, she raised her eyes beneath closed eyelids, trying to discover the undiscoverable: Would her child and husband survive? Allowing her mind to drift to her childhood years, she now viewed her life from a completely different angle. How many times had she had difficult moments? How many times did she think she'd never make it out of a hole? In the same way she had believed that she would emerge from sorrowful times, Isabella was determined to stay strong and have faith that her family would succeed. Would she be able to bring them back? This remained a mystery.

Chapter 30

❧ • ❧

With all her might, Kate climbed up the scarf her father held above. While she pulled and tugged, her father held on to it tightly. Kate was persistent and put a tremendous amount of effort into her climb. No longer was it mere desire to succeed; it had morphed into a mandate! She was almost there, almost back with her father. Every drop of sweat, which ironically slid down her forehead signified another dismaying emotion buried deep within her heart. There she was searching for security and confidence, and every step of the way she exercised her strength to reach the platform rock. She aggressively grabbed onto it and tossed the scarf to the ground.

Yes! Kate thought to herself.

Yet another time, she heard her father say, "It's not for you to finish." Smiling knowingly, he added, "I told you that we would be able to succeed." Feeling every inch of her bones shake in exhaustion, Kate recalled the frightening moments she had just endured. She also thought of dreams she wished she had never dreamt, ones where she was walking up a rickety stairway, clueless about what awaited her at the top. She felt afraid.

Why do I have to add fear to my already treacherous hardships? Kate wondered. She just wished for mercy, if only a little. Lifting her head in courage and certainty, she began trudging again. Destined to carry this solemn burden, she felt that she had no other choice.

"I can clearly see the peak!" Kate said through frigid lips, a glimmer of hope in her eyes. At the top of the rocky mountain, she saw the peak standing proudly amid rays of sunshine. There seemed to be an object on the peak. As she and her father tried to make out what it was, Kate felt pressed for time, so she resumed climbing the volcano with more might than ever. Thinking that they were almost there, they heard a trembling hiss coming from the rocks around them. Fear crept up their spines. At a loss for how to react, their first instinct was to freeze, but there was no time for that. Gregorio glanced at his watch. They desperately needed to keep moving. Placing their terror aside, they continued hiking towards the peak.

"Don't give up, darling. We will make it," Gregorio said in a comforting tone.

The sound of her father's comfort and care stamped itself in Kate's heart. She hadn't heard her father speak with sincerity for what seemed like forever, although it had just been several hours.

"Thank you, Father," Kate said, warm tear of joy sliding down her cheek and onto the shiny necklace she had received for her 11th birthday. The number 11 is cursed. People of some cultures believe that it leaves a mark on a person. Kate worried that it would negatively imprint her heart. Belief was what kept her strong and determined to think positive thoughts.

Still yearning to reach the mountaintop, Kate and her father heard the hiss grow louder. They feared that their hopes would be shattered. Feeling a breeze brush their cheeks, they knew it wasn't a natural phenomenon but a gust of hopelessness that washed away their expectations.

"Where is the thing that is making that noise?" Kate asked, shaking her head in fear. A shadow slipped between her feet. She didn't know where to look or where to hide. It was just her out there as she felt all alone.

With every step that Gregorio attempted
to take, every time he shifted, he knew that
the sound was made up of more than starving
snakes. It was also the sound of trepidation, the
thumping of his daughter's heart. In addition to
the unpleasant sound that haunted them, there
was an odious odor. The sour scent of worry
and anxiety thickened the air, making Kate and
Gregorio's already unbearable journey even
more agonizing. Their precious faith—a slim
thread balanced between life and death—was
shaking. They felt threatened and frightened
as the noise came closer. Feeling confused, they
had nowhere to turn for help, nowhere to hide.
The sound surrounded them. Moments later, the
snakes appeared and encircled them! Sliding
from side to side, the snakes used their long,
deadly tongues to hiss and their sharp tails to
rattle. Kate and her father panicked. The snakes
twirled themselves around the Tyler's. As Kate's
eyes tingled in alarm, she searched for a way out
of the lethal situation. As the seconds passed, she
began to choke. Her skin turned different shades
of blue before turning green. It seemed as though
the snakes spent their time trying to survive, as
well. Slowly making their way up and around
the Tyler's' bodies, the snakes hissed, the sound
entered deep into Kate and Gregorio's ears and
becoming part of them. The fear of losing time

tormented them. Their heads pounding, they seemed stuck in the moment, but the faint sound of a ticking clock made them both cry. Those tears symbolized more than just pain and regret; they also indicated anger. Gregorio's urge to save his family was as immeasurable as his love for them. With adrenaline pumping through his body, he found the strength to cast off the snakes that had looped around his body. It required no act of magic. The look on Kate's face was haunting. Her eyeballs seemed ready to pop out of her head. She was drained. Saliva slid from her lip. If Gregorio didn't do something quickly, he would lose her. With great might, he ripped the snakes away from his daughter. Leaving her on the ground to catch her breath, he threw the snakes off the volcano. The sight of them flying in mid air triggered an emotion of contentment he hadn't experienced in a while. The sound of their hissing no longer frightened him; now, it was music to his ears. Wiping his sweaty forehead, he turned to find Kate missing from the spot on the ground where he had laid her. Inhaling deeply in frustration, he lifted his eyes in desperation until, from the corner of his eye, he spied Kate running up the mountain in complete distress and fatigue.

"There's only two minutes left. *Quick!*" she hollered.

Rushing to his daughter's side, Gregorio glared at his watch as the seconds passed. Carrying his heavy bag made his climb all the more difficult. He felt that he was dragging himself up the volcano.

"Look, it's so close," Kate said to her father while pointing to a black flag. Nodding his head in exasperation, he motioned to her not to waste time. Just run. Their future was now in *her* hands.

*   *   *

"How can this be? According to my calculations, the volcano is supposed to come to life, shake, let out its lava and burn them! What is happening? They're not supposed to make it!" Ednesto shouted to the weak Isabella who was tied up beside him. As frail and as pale as she was, nothing stopped her from smiling. G-d was with her child and husband. Exhaling loudly in frustration, Ednesto seemed unable to accept the possibility that Kate and Gregorio would make it. He clutched his hands together and roared. As father and daughter both turned to face the volcano, Ednesto's face beamed as he whispered, *"Yes."*

*　　*　　*

"*Kate?!*" Gregorio yelled with all his might to his daughter.

"Daddy, what's happening?" she fervently asked while looking down the shaky mountainside. "Let's hope it doesn't erupt in the next minute and 50 seconds. We need to place our hands on that flag!"

Continuing their journey up the mountain, they dragged their bodies, fighting against the agitated volcano that was about to vent and release its lava. At the present moment, Kate could think of nothing better to describe this task—and the concomitant love in her heart for her family—than the words of Bruce Lee: "Love is like a friendship caught on fire. In the beginning a flame, very pretty, often hot and fierce, but still only light and flickering. As love grows older, our hearts mature and our love becomes as coals, deep-burning and unquenchable."

With only love on her mind, Kate couldn't possibly acknowledge the fact that there were fewer than two minutes remaining—and that she and her father still had not made it the top.

Once her father reached her side, he gently caressed her hand. Grinning, she looked up to see a frightful sight. Her father's pupils were practically drowning. Kate knew that this was not good.

At this point, all they could do was run and hope to reach the top on in time. Running with all their might, they made it! Inhaling breathlessly, they both looked at their watches at the same time: they had three seconds left. As they both reached out their hands to grab the flag to break the curse, they felt as if a burden were being lifted from their chests. It was actually happening, the moment they were waiting for. All the suffering and pain was finally coming to an end. As Kate's delicate hand touched the soft flag, the volcano rumbled. Soon enough, it pushed her to the ground. *One more second,* she thought to herself. *I can't let this happen.* Determined to succeed, she got back to her feet and stood beside the flag. Once again, the ground rumbled. The volcano erupted. Lava began spilling from all sides. It seemed as though this were Niagara Falls—and it had turned to flame. Flying rocks increased the danger. *That's it,* Kate thought, knowing that she had lost an amazing mother. As tears began rolling down Kate's face, she searched for her father while protecting her head from the rocks and fire. Ducking and running, she needed her father by her side. As she searched in all directions, her eyes locked with what seemed to be an illusion of Ednesto's. Kate shook her head in disgust and pain. Ednesto nodded in joy.

She read his lips, which said, "I possess it; all the magic is in my hands." These words confirmed that Kate's mother was dead. She continued scanning the landscape in search of her father. Finally, fearful and saddened, she saw him lying on the ground. Blood was gushing all over his body. Kate froze in fear. A heavy rock fell on her left arm and fractured the bone. Ignoring the terrible pain, she ran towards her father. Just then, an angry wind rolled in and stopped her from making progress. Then, the gust flung her father up into the air. Her eyes met his for a second before he disappeared into the volcano. Kate was about to run after him just as she heard a commotion. It was a rescue team. A helicopter soon appeared over her head.

A man rappelled down a knotted rope and grabbed Kate just after she had yelled, *"No!"* Her painful echo remained on the mountain. Some say that it can be heard to this day.

Chapter 31

From the moment she boarded the helicopter, Kate had felt woozy. A gigantic hole had appeared in her fragile heart. Every time she had a pleasant thought about her family, the hole expanded. The thought of being sent away to an orphanage was horrible; she couldn't bear the fact that she was all alone. Going through the 11 hours had felt like the worst thing that a person could endure, but Kate had learned since then that the worst possible thing was to lose both her parents. She pinched herself frequently, desperately hoping that she had only been dreaming. Before now, the thought of losing both her parents had never even entered her mind. Looking through the helicopter windscreen and down at the flaming fire, she fervently searched for her father, even if only to see his lifeless body. He was the only thing left in her life, the only thing that mattered to her. The thought of finding herself all alone in an empty house frightened her. With no siblings, aunts or cousins, Kate legitimately felt abandoned. As the thought sank in, it was too much for her 11-year-old self. She passed out. Sometime later, she awoke to find herself hooked to a respirator and lying in a hospital bed. She felt a jolt in her bones and was too frightened to keep her eyes open. The doctors surrounding Kate terrified. Their masked faces led her to cry dramatically and shriek vividly.

"Get me home. I want to leave!" she heard her weak voice roar, after having removed the respirator tube. As if choreographed, each doctor turned, alarmed.

"Looks like she woke up," one of the doctors said as he removed his latex gloves. Nodding in confirmation, Kate began wiping away her tears. The doctor spoke to her.

"We understand what you're going through. We're really sorry. The hospital is trying its best to get you into the best home . . ." He paused and looked around at the other doctors, who nodded their heads. He could see that the girl was terrified, but he could do nothing more than continue to comfort her. "We—"

"Wait, but what about Ednesto? What happened to him?" Kate interrupted the moment she was able to catch her breath and utter a few words.

"I'm sorry, I'm not sure I know who you're talking about," the doctor said in confusion, feeling bad that he wasn't able to help her. Kate's face turned several shades of red, first in anger and then in embarrassment. Moments later, when she regained her composure, she asked again, this time trying to clarify as much as possible.

"Ednesto. He was the mastermind behind this entire thing. He's the one who killed my mother and my father. The tower . . ." Kate said through her teeth. She was frustrated, trying to get her point across but mumbling and stammering. The doctors felt bad that they weren't able to assist her.

"What happened to the tower?" Kate managed to ask through purple lips. A long moment of silence ensued.

One of the doctors adjusted himself in his seat and said slowly,

"Everything surrounding the volcano burned." He paused for a few moments and then resumed. "Yes, even the tower," he said in a stable voice, uncertain whether Kate would take this news as good or bad. Sure that nothing would stop Ednesto from escaping, Kate fumed at the thought that he was still out there living a happy life with his *magic.*

"In fact," another doctor said, "the only thing recovered from the scene was this bag." He then gently took Kate's backpack from beneath his chair. At the sight of her backpack, Kate's heart skipped a beat. All her precious belongings were in there: her journal, her camera, her accessories—and, of course, the music box. Desperately yearning to find out what had become of her mother, Kate now needed to know whether or not the box still played music. She inhaled deeply, and began pleading with the doctors to release her from the hospital. For a while they remained stubborn, until after hours of work she managed to talk them into letting her for a long stroll. She quickly jumped out of the bed and headed straight to the alarmed doctor across the room. Once standing before him, she paused.

"I appreciate all you did for me until now, Thank you."

After delivering her emotional good-bye, she grabbed the backpack and ran out of the hospital. Determining her exact location, she calculated. If she ran fast enough, she would make it to her house in 14 minutes. Running and gasping, Kate felt a shadow cross her head. She became afraid, shaking and thinking this was another horrid experience she would have to go through, another occurrence that would add yet one more sour drop to her already full cup. Looking up in fear, she was glad to discover that the shadow was only a cloud, albeit a heavy one. In a matter of seconds, it began pouring rain. Drenched, nothing would stop Kate from running. Precisely 14 minutes later, she reached her house. Looking through her backpack for her keys, she noticed the music box once again. Adrenaline passed through her body. She aggressively scanned her bag for her keys. Once inside the house, she looked around and collapsed to the ground in horror.

I will never again see my mother walk through the kitchen with a delicious supper in her hands. Never again will I see my father come home from work smiling, eager to spend time with his family, Kate thought, wiping the moisture from her face. She couldn't tell if it was soaked from her tears or from the rain. Lying on the floor, she heard a gentle voice say her name. She jumped in fear and rapidly raced up the stairs.

"Oh, Kate, I'm so glad to see you." Catherine rushed over and embraced her. Seeing her loyal nanny made Kate smile, but she couldn't speak. The look on Kate's face revealed practically everything she had gone through. Understanding that Kate was having difficulty coping, Catherine left her alone to grieve. After running to her room, Kate emptied her backpack on her bed to find *the box*. Placing it on her knees, she opened the lid, frantically hoping to hear music. Once fully opened, the box was silent. Lowering her head in sadness, Kate jumped onto her bed. She needed to sleep, to escape from the world. Feeling sodden, she knew that she wouldn't be able to fall asleep. She decided to take a shower, hoping that afterwards she would feel better. That wasn't to be so, however. Hoping that a good drowse would help, she buried her head in her pillow.

Upon waking four hours later, Kate felt worse than ever. She finally understood that nothing would ease her pain. Grieving is something that many people don't understand unless they experience it themselves. When a family member dies, a part of you dies, too.

Still trying to regain her composure and face reality, Kate couldn't help but weep. After an hour of overpowering sorrow, she felt that her eyes must surely run out of tears. With hot, red cheeks, Kate lay on her bed and concentrated on the small music box on the floor beside it. She wished that the heavy lump in her throat would vanish. Perhaps a cold glass of milk would help. Despite the fact that she had no appetite, Kate slowly made her way down the stairs, focusing on every move she made, calculating her every action. Once down the steps, she hurried to the fridge to retrieve her glass of milk. As she poured the cold milk into a cup, she felt as though an oasis had just appeared before her eyes. Sitting down at kitchen table, memories played in her mind—unforgettable moments, both good and bad. As the cold milk slid down her throat, she heard a bizarre sound. Slowly placing the cup on the table, she looked around in confusion. Momentarily, she saw something from the corner of her eye. The doorknob was turning. Sure she was dreaming, she rubbed her eyes. Seeing that the knob continued moving, Kate felt her heart skip a beat. The door opened a crack. Afraid, Kate wasn't sure if she wanted to know who was standing behind that door. In a few moments, she found out.

Kate's mother and father walked through the door, both of them wearing enormous smiles.

The moment Kate saw them, her eyes widened and her cheeks reddened. Not expecting to see her parents ever again, Kate was shocked. She didn't think she had the strength to handle it. Her lips began to part as she searched for the right words to say to her 'resurrected' parents. Her pupils began to swim as the corner of her eye caught sight of the golden horn clutched between her father's fingers. Slightly confused, Kate saw her father nodding at her, as if he knew exactly what she was thinking. Yes, this was the horns mysterious power!

CPSIA information can be obtained at www.ICGtesting.com
Printed in the USA
LVOW06s1440200814

400097LV00001B/23/P

9 781496 912343